Lock Down Publications and Ca$h
Presents

I0664150

Thug of Spades 3
Cemetery Gates

Written By
Corey Robinson

First Edition 2024

Printed in the United States of America

Lock Down Publications
P.O. Box 944
Stockbridge, GA 30281
www.lockdownpublications.com

Like our page on Facebook: Lock Down Publications
www.facebook.com/lockdownpublications.ldp

Stay Connected with Us!

Text **LOCKDOWN** to 22828 to stay up-to-date with new releases, sneak peaks, contests and more…

Like our page on Facebook:
Lock Down Publications

Join Lock Down Publications/The New Era Reading Group

Visit our website:
www.lockdownpublications.com

Follow us on Instagram:
Lock Down Publications

Email Us: We want to hear from you!

A coward dies a thousand deaths.
A soldier dies but once.

~Bryann T
(Who Told You)

Chapter 1

Dreighton Myers sat on the thin mattress and stared at the white, barren cement walls that had housed him for four years. To some, that may have been a short time, but to Dre, it seemed like forever. He listened to the footsteps that echoed down the hall and prepared himself. Everything he owned sat in a small metal locker in the corner of the room and that was where it would remain. Dre had no more use for it so he decided to leave it behind for the next man that would sit in his spot.

When the mechanical door slid open, Dre looked up into the eyes of the guard who would escort him to freedom. The small man was old enough to be his grandfather and when Dre stood, he towered over but him the man was not intimidated. He had been a guard at the prison for over twenty years and had dealt with many hardened criminals. It took him years to gain their respect but once he got it, he kept it.

Dre nodded and stepped out of the cell and then followed the guard down the long hallway. His chest swelled with nervousness and anticipation at the same time. He had waited for that very moment for so long and yet, there he was, not sure he was even ready.

Dre looked straight ahead while the other inmates stood at their doors and watched him pass. One day, their time would come too, but that day was his, and he didn't want to share it with anybody. Dre hadn't been successful at making friends since he had been there but having friends didn't matter to him. He felt like they would all turn into enemies anyway. He had also become accustomed to hanging by himself because he had done it for so long.

"Alright, Myers, go ahead and sign your papers. You are now a free man. Good luck out there. It's been a pleasure knowing you." The old guard smiled and turned around so he could walk back to his station.

For some reason, him leaving bothered Dre, but he shook it off. He had gotten used to people walking out of his life and leaving him to fend for himself, but that shit only made him stronger. Besides, he didn't have time to dwell on the past or on those who had abandoned him.

As soon as Dre signed his release papers, thoughts of his mother came to mind. Things on the outside would feel strange without her. He was still trying to wrap his feelings around her being dead. Kiara had never given a damn about him but somehow, deep in the pits of his heart, he still held love for her. She had given him life, albeit, a miserable one, but it was life all the same.

Dre folded up his release papers and put them in the pocket of the jeans he had picked out of the prison's donation box. He had been lucky to find a decent T-shirt and a pair of no name brand shoes to match. His father had sent him an EOS box, but he had refused it and sent it back. He knew that Daymion was only trying to be a good father, but Dre didn't need the hospitality. He just wanted to do his time and move the fuck on. Dre had told his pops that he didn't want any visitors while he was locked up, but Daymion showed up anyway, along with Kayla and sometimes Tasha, but Dre refused every visit. He figured that after all the time Daymion had done behind the walls, he would understand, but instead he went every weekend in hopes that Dre would change his mind, but he was a Myers, and their word was their bond.

The release officer handed Dre a prepaid fifty-dollar debit card and resource information but then turned and walked away to answer a call. Dre wondered why he hadn't been given a bus ticket but didn't want to stick around to ask. His two feet worked just fine and when he walked out of the last set of doors, he inhaled as much air as he could. Somehow, the taste of it was different than that on the inside. It seemed clearer and more refreshing and caused him to close his eyes and bask in its glory. He had been so lost in the ambience of it all but when a familiar voice called his name, he instantly snapped out of it. He opened his eyes and scrunched his eyebrows together. He couldn't believe what he was seeing but there it was, staring right back at him.

"What's the matter, Dre? You look like you done seen a ghost."

Dre looked Tasha up and down. She wasn't the same girl he remembered from four years earlier. Her hair was no longer nappy and untamed but instead, hung in long curls down the middle of her back. Her cocoa-colored skin was smooth and flawless and even without makeup, she looked picture ready. Her glossed, full lips shined like a diamond in the sun and made Dre wonder how they would feel on his. He felt his dick pulsate at the sight of her and if it wouldn't have been for his t-shirt, she would have noticed that she had his manhood on swole. He felt like he should play shit cool, at least until he figured out where her mind was at.

"Damn, Tasha. I almost ain't recognize your ass. You done grew the fuck up. The hell is you doing out here anyway?"

"Uh, duh. I'm here to pick you up, Dre. I know you couldn't have possibly thought that I would let you take a bus."

"I would have been cool with taking a bus, but they ain't give me no damn bus ticket. How you even know that I was getting released today?"

"Come on now, Dre, just because you didn't want to be bothered by anyone while you were in there didn't mean shit. I still kept tabs on you the entire time."

"Yeah. Well, I'm sorry about that, but when you and your grandma came to see me that first time, it fucked me up real hard when you all left. I wouldn't have been able to go through that mental shit all the time, so I thought it was best to just do me and forget about what I had left out here."

"I guess I can understand your logic, but how do you think that made us feel?"

"I couldn't live in here and out there too, Tasha. I had to let one of them go. Shit just made it easier."

"Well, I forgive you and so does everybody else. Now come on so we can go get you something decent to put on."

"What's wrong with what I got on?"

"Boy, please. You can't walk around looking like you just came from a homeless shelter. You're the son of a king, so you need to dress like one."

"Whatever, Tasha."

The comment made Dre think about his father as he followed behind Tasha. He made sure to stay a few steps back so he could watch her fat ass as she walked. He felt like she knew he was looking because she slung her hips extra hard. Dre had to admit that he liked what he saw. He was so focused on her ass that when she came to a stop, he lightly bumped into her. Tasha just giggled and shook her head.

Dre raised his eyebrows when he realized that she had stopped at a rose gold Benz. He wondered how she had been able to afford such luxury because last he remembered, she was broke except for the little bit of money Kenny would slide her when she would make runs. He thought about Kenny but didn't inquire, because honestly, Kenny was dead to him.

"Nice car, but I know you ain't come to pick me up in another nigga's ride."

"Uh-uh, Dre. This beauty is all mine. And if you want to know if I have a man, all you gotta do is ask."

Dre didn't even respond to the comment. He didn't want Tasha to know that the thought of another man being close to her fucked with him real hard. He had to give credit where it was due. She had weathered the storm with him and never shut the umbrella even though he had paid her no mind when he was free. He had been so caught up in trying to impress Shay that he didn't see the diamond in the rough that had been right in front of him the whole time.

"Nah, that ain't my business. You grown and can do what you want to do. I'm just making sure that you ain't putting me in some drama."

"Come on, Dre. You should know by now that I would never put you in a fucked-up position. You got me confused with that other bitch."

"So, I see you still hatin' on Shay. You need to let that little girl shit go."

"Hating? That hoe ain't shit to hate on. She's the one who left you for dead inside those cement walls and ran off with her daddy. Even after all he put you through, that bitch had the nerve to show him some damn loyalty. That was real fucked up how she did you, Dre. She don't deserve a nigga like you."

"And you do?"

"You damn right I do, and I ain't never going anywhere, so you better open your eyes and realize who has your back. Besides your father and Kayla, I'm all you got."

Tasha turned around and opened her car door with an attitude. She looked back at Dre with tears in her eyes, got in the car and shut the door behind her. Dre knew that she had mad love for him and would ride with him until the bitter end, but he wanted better for her. He was headed down a path of destruction and he couldn't afford to chance her being caught in the crossfire. Dre thought that after all the years he had been gone, she would have moved on, but Tasha was solid and had stuck in there.

Dre shrugged his shoulders and walked around to the other side of her car and got in. The inside of the Benz was just as clean as the outside. His weight sunk right into the soft leather seat as if it had been custom made just for him. He couldn't lie, he was impressed and proud at the same time. Tasha had come a long way and as much as he wanted to speak, he felt like it would be best if he waited for her to start up a conversation. He knew how females got when they were in their feelings. He was just ready to get off the prison grounds and move on with his mission. Dre swore that he wouldn't rest until he found Malachi Jenson. He owed him, not only for the shit he put him through, but for the death of his mother. She didn't deserve to die, no matter what she had done.

The sound of the car purring to life shook Dre from his thoughts and brought him back to reality. He leaned his seat back and stretched his legs out so he could relax during the ride, but when the car didn't move, he pulled the lever and brought the seat back up.

"The fuck is up, Tasha? Why the hell we still sitting in this damn parking lot?"

"Get the hell outta my car, Dre!"

"What? Girl stop trippin and let's go."

"Nigga, I'm not tripping. Get out."

"And how am I supposed to get home?"

"Walk your black ass there, or better yet, take the bus like you wanted to do in the first place."

Dre shook his head and got out of Tasha's ride. As soon as he shut the door behind him, she backed out of the parking spot and drove away. Dre stood there for a minute and tried to process what had just happened and still, he couldn't believe it. He was ready to get away from that hell hole, so he put one foot in front of the other and walked. He was thankful that he didn't have anything to carry because he had enough weight on his shoulders already.

No sooner than he turned down the road that left to the main highway, Tasha pulled up beside him and let her window down. "Don't ever question anything about me and my feelings when it comes to you, now get in so we can go celebrate your release."

Dre hesitated but eventually walked around and got back inside the vehicle. He had always been told that women were something else when it came to their feelings, and now, he had experienced it firsthand. He felt like it would be best if he played things off as if it had never happened, but soon realized it wouldn't go as planned.

"So, what you mean by celebrate? What you got in mind?"

"Dre, don't try to act like shit is cool between us right now. You know where my head is at with you, and yet you still treat me like an outcast. I've played second to that bitch Shay for years and dammit, I'm not doing it anymore. My feelings for you are valid and you can't expect me to walk away when I've come so far with you. I deserve you. I'm all the way in and if I got to kill that bitch to prove a point, I will."

"Whoa, Tasha, the fuck is you talking about killing someone for? Shit ain't even going to come to that. I got your point, but right now, a woman ain't my focus. I'm trying to get at that mufucka that took my momma's life. When that's taken care of, then I can concentrate on other shit."

Tasha softened her attitude at the mention of Dre's mother. She felt bad that Kiara had been killed and even worse that he didn't have a chance to tell her goodbye.

"I'm sorry about your mother, and even after all the hell she put you through, you still got love for her. That's what I admire most about you. I don't know if I could do it like that."

11

"All bullshit aside, she gave me life, and for that, I owe her."

"What about your father, Dre? Don't you think you should stop pushing fault on him and build something solid with what you got left?"

"Don't worry, Tasha. Me and my pops is gone be straight. Just got some shit we need to work through; that's all."

Tasha nodded and put her focus back on the drive ahead of her. She put in a Toosii CD and bobbed her head to the beat of *Favorite Song*, which really was her favorite because she felt like he was singing right to her. The rest of the ride would be a smooth one. Tasha was dealing with her own inner thoughts while Dre sat back and stole small glances at her. He wondered how he had gotten lucky enough to have her by his side. One day, he would reward her greatly for the loyalty she had shown him, but first, he would need to let go of the past and the only way to do that would be to find Shay and get some type of closure. The only problem was, he had no idea where to start looking for her. Ever since she left town with Malachi, she had been a ghost, but Dre was determined to find her and her father, and he would not stop looking until he found them.

Dre had been lost in his thoughts when he felt the car come to a stop. He looked out of his window and saw the bright lights that lit up the mall's parking lot. Since his mind had been on other things during the ride, he didn't realize how long the drive had really been. Dusk had begun to settle in the sky, telling the world that it would soon be filled with darkness. It felt like it had been forever since Dre had seen a night sky and he was anxious to take it all in. It almost seemed unreal, and he had to pinch himself to make sure he wasn't in a dream. He was really free, and it felt damn good; better than anything else he had ever experienced.

"Hey, what you thinking about over there?"

"Just feels good to see the darkness coming in. I was always in my cell at this time of day, so a sunset would only be something I could imagine."

"I guess you don't really miss the small things until they're no longer in your reach. Makes you appreciate it a little more once you have it again."

"Yeah, well, I'm glad it's you that I'm sharing this moment with, and I know I haven't thanked you for hanging in there with me through all of this bullshit, but you have to know that I do appreciate you and how loyal you have been to me; even going against your own blood. That shit is real, and I owe you everything for that."

"No, Dre. You don't owe me anything. For you, I'd go through it all over again if I had to."

"Well, you ain't gonna have to do that because a nigga is trying to remain free."

Tasha smiled because she couldn't agree more. She couldn't imagine Dre being gone another four years, but she also had to live with the fact that he had murder and mayhem on his mind. She wanted to have as much time with him as she could because dealing with Dre, tomorrow wasn't promised. She thought about trying to convince him to let the shit with Malachi go but felt like that would be too much to ask, especially knowing that he killed Dre's mother in cold blood. Whatever payback Dre had planned for him would be well deserved and she would be there to have his back every step of the way.

Dre's paranoia kicked in as soon as he stepped into the mall. It had been a long time since he had been in a crowded area, and it had him on edge. When he was on the inside, he had his own space and niggas knew to respect it. He had been afraid to leave out of his cell too much, not because he feared what someone might do to him but because of what he had a mind to do to them. His hurt and anger had been so deep that anyone could have been a victim of his rage, so he decided it was best to stay to himself. He couldn't afford to let anything hinder his release.

Dre stood still and looked around at all the other patrons, and even though they seemed to be in their own world, he still couldn't trust it. He suddenly felt a hand grip his and remembered that he wasn't alone. When he heard Tasha's voice, it somehow soothed his spirit and made him feel less tense. It truly amazed him how she knew something was wrong. She had always been in tune with him and his thoughts, but Dre wasn't sure if that was a good or bad thing. I guess in time, he would find out.

"Come on, Dre. We can go somewhere else. Somewhere that's not so busy."

"Nah, I'm good. Just gotta ease back into life slowly. That's all."

Dre smiled a half smile at her and then squeezed her hand tightly. Together, they walked deeper into the mall. Dre stayed on alert and watched everyone who passed him because he felt like they were watching him too. Doing time in the pen made him feel more anxious than he had ever been, and it caused him to wonder if his father had the same issue when he had gotten out. He would make sure to ask him.

Tasha pulled Dre toward an urban clothing store, and he made sure to check out his surroundings as soon as they entered. He eased up some when he noticed there were only a few customers. He locked eyes with the female behind the counter and nodded a what's up to her. She smiled at him flirtatiously and held her cell phone up, hinting that she wanted his number so they could hook up, but Dre had never been one to jump on the pussy band wagon and he wasn't about to start. As a matter of fact, he had never even been inside of a pussy. There were many times his dick had gotten hard around Shay, but the opportunity to give it to her had never come. Dre wasn't ashamed of the fact that he was still a virgin but he couldn't wait to get his dick wet so he could see what all the fuss was about.

"You see anything you like, Dre? You can have whatever you want. Your father already has a closet full of outfits and shoes for you, but you know I gotta look out, too."

The mention of his father made Dre feel a little emotional. He knew he had been wrong for dismissing him, but Dre needed time to figure shit out and clear his mind. It just took him four years to do it. He believed that since Daymion had done some time, he would understand and respect that shit but he had done the opposite and showed up every weekend. Dre knew he was trying to make up for lost time, but his refusing visits didn't hinder Daymion one bit. Dre wondered why he hadn't been with Tasha to pick him up, but instead of asking, he came to his own conclusion.

After some browsing, Dre found a few outfits and some kicks he liked. He had never been materialistic, so he didn't try to take advantage of the situation. He also didn't know how deep Tasha's pockets were although she had told him to get whatever he wanted. Driving a Benz didn't mean shit because some people did it just for show. They would be pushing a nice ass ride and still be living in a Section 8 apartment. Dre made sure to tread lightly on the dollar amount he spent just in case.

When he had got what he wanted, he carried the goods to the counter and laid them down. The cashier slid her cell phone close to him before ringing the merchandise up. However, the move didn't go unnoticed by Tasha, who slammed her black card on the counter causing the girl behind it to jump. Dre might not have been Tasha's man, but a bitch was going to respect her mind when she was with him.

Dre raised his eyebrows and let out a stifled laugh but somehow knew better than to say anything. He figured it would be best to let Tasha handle the situation. He had to admit though, the chick was cute, but he was almost certain that she slid her phone to every nigga that came through. Dre had enough problems and didn't have the time or energy to waste on an easy bitch, plus, he needed loyalty and was sure that she didn't understand what that word meant.

The girl rolled her eyes at Tasha but somehow knew not to say anything. When she gave her back her credit card, she smiled a fake smile and bagged up the items and then slid the bag across the counter. Dre didn't even bother to thank her before grabbing the bag and turning to leave with Tasha on his heels. He glanced back just in time to see the cashier check her phone with a look of disappointment on her face. She didn't know that he had just been released from the pen and didn't have a number to give her, but he would leave her to her own thoughts about it.

"The fuck is you able to afford a black card?"

"Sorry to disappoint you, Dre, but like I said before, I'm not that same little girl that used to run behind you and Kenny. There is so much you don't know about me. Things you would have learned long ago had you not been running behind that nothing ass bitch."

"Now, come on, Tasha. Cut the girl some slack. Shay ain't never did shit to you. Besides, I'm here with you now, not her."

"Yeah, you are, but only by default. I'm sure if you were given a choice, you would be with her, but as long as I got air in my lungs, that ain't gonna happen."

"And when was you gone tell me that you running shit?"

"I just did."

Dre wasn't about to argue with her about her position because in all actuality, she was running the show. He had been gone for four years and needed to get his status up before he could claim to be a boss. However, he had other things he needed to handle first. Silence filled the car as Dre sat back and watched the passing traffic until suddenly, his mother came to mind. He wished that he could have somehow save her. No one knew it, but Dre often blamed himself for her death. He felt that if he hadn't killed the wrong man, she would still be alive. He hated the fact that he actually missed her. He tried but couldn't get her face out of his vision. He knew she would remain there until he gave her some closure.

"Take me to see her."

"What? Don't try me like that, Dre. Even if we both knew where she was, I wouldn't take you to see the bitch."

"I'm not talking about Shay, so get off that shit. I'm talking about my mother. I need to go see her, Tasha. I got some shit on my chest that I need to get off."

"Um, don't you think it would be best if you got your father to take you instead?"

"Nah, the shit I need to say is between me and her. Me and my pops can deal with what we got going on at another time. Besides, I doubt he would want to waste his energy like that. He ain't got that type of love for her."

"Look, Dre, I don't know the whole story that your parents shared, but I'm sure he holds some kind of love for her. If for no other reason, for giving him, you. You gotta believe that. Anyway, I told him that I was going to pick you up and take you straight home. We have already used up a lot of time with the shopping and all, so I think I should take you home."

"I'm not a child, Tasha. I'm a grown fucking man and I follow my own rules. You obviously don't understand, but I need to go see her. You can take me to pops house afterwards. This is something I got to do, so you can either support my decision and take me, or I'll find another way to get there. Your choice."

Tasha had vowed to always have Dre's back and wanted to live up to her word, so she slowed down and turned at the next light. She would glance at him every few minutes and could tell the thoughts of his mother was weighing him down. She wondered how he would feel after he visited the grave site where she had been buried. Tasha thought back to how Kiara had treated her only child and now, it was too late for her to make things right.

Dre sat up in his seat as soon as she turned into the cemetery. Tasha could sense his nervousness but said nothing. As soon as she parked and cut the engine off, Dre turned to look at her. He was scared and she knew it. She could read the pain and confusion that he held in his eyes and hoped that after he said what he had to say to his mother, the burden he carried would go away.

"Stay in the car. I need to do this by myself. I won't be long."

Tasha only nodded in response. She understood Dre more than anyone else. She sat as still as she could as he got out of the car and lightly shut the door behind him. His heart pounded in anticipation of what he was about to do. He walked down the row of graves and for some reason, read the name off of each one of them out loud. He wondered how those people had died and how often the people that loved them came to visit and pay their respect, he also wondered how many of them never got fresh flowers and how it would feel to be lying beside them. He continued to walk down the line of headstones until he got to the one that bore his mother's name. Kiara Taylor. Dre stood still and stared at it for a moment before dropping to his knees, in front of it. He ran his fingers over the letters and swore he could feel her presence. She knew he was there. She had been waiting for him and he would finally give her the peace she needed to rest.

"Sup, ma? It's me, Dreighton. I know you been waiting for me to come see you and I'm sorry it took me so long, but I had to wait for them crackas to let me go. I'm here now, though, and I need to let you know that I ain't mad at you for anything. I just wish I could understand why you hated me so much when I ain't neva had nothing but love for you. I know you wished that love would have come from pops, but I had enough to cover the both of us, still do. I'm sorry I couldn't protect you. I just wasn't strong enough to handle that nigga, but I done got my weight up and I'ma get at that mufucka that got at you. I give you my word on that. Just make sure you save me a spot beside you. Rest in peace, ma."

Dre kissed the tip of his fingers and then pressed them to her name. He stood up with a different attitude and walked away. He was about to wreak havoc in the hood until someone gave him some answers. It was time to bring Malachi Jenson out of hiding and Dre was determined to be waiting for him. Malachi owed him and he was ready to be paid, even if it cost him his life.

Chapter 2

Daymion Myers stood on the balcony of the lavish home he had purchased for him and Kayla. The view was breathtaking and one you could usually only find in expensive magazines because it had been meant only for the elite.

He had been in deep thought when he felt Kayla wrap her arms around his waist and hug him from behind, a habit she had that he truly adored. Daymion was grateful that she had forgiven him for not reaching out to her when he had been released from prison after doing close to a dub. It wasn't that he didn't want to contact her, but he'd had some beef he needed to handle and didn't want to involve her in the drama, but as soon as he finished taking care of those issues, he went to her and explained his reasons. Thankfully, she understood and welcomed him with open arms and a loving heart. The rest was history.

"What are you out here thinking about?"

Daymion turned around to face the woman he loved. He had never been the real mushy type, but Kayla had managed to change something deep inside of him. Something that he thought no woman could ever do. Out in the streets, Daymion ruled with a fist of steel, but at home with her, he was like a slab of ice that had been sitting out in the blazing sun. She was it for him and he knew it, so he cherished every single moment spent with her as if it would be his last.

"Honestly, I was out here thinking about Kiara. Dre will be here soon, and I know he's going to ask a lot of questions. Ones that I'm not going to want to answer. I've been such a disappointment to him all of his life and her getting murdered at the hands of the enemy only adds to that load."

"Come on, Day. Dre knows that Kiara being killed was not your fault. I'm sure if you would have known he had a target on her head, you would have prevented it. Her blood is on Malachi's hands, not yours. So, you need to stop carrying that weight around on your shoulders."

"I know Kayla, but I still feel somewhat responsible, and I'll carry that burden until I put Jensen six feet deep. The ground is where he deserves to be."

"And what if he never gets put in the ground? What if he never comes out of hiding? You have to stop dwelling on him and his whereabouts because it is consuming your every thought. Dre will be home, and you can finally make up for all the time you two have lost. Don't let that drama with Malachi interfere with what you have waited so long for."

Daymion knew that Kayla was right, but how could she expect him to rest knowing that Malachi Jensen was out there somewhere still breathing? Daymion felt like it was his duty to avenge Kiara's death. How could he not? Regardless of how he felt about her, she was the mother of his son, and she deserved to rest in peace. Justice for her would be served, street style.

"Look, I give you my word that how I feel about this will not disturb anything I try to establish with Dre. Building a bond with him will be my number one priority. You have nothing to be worried about."

"I really hope you mean it because Dre has had it pretty rough, and he's going to need you to be a solid force in his life. He's going to need stability because Kiara never gave it to him. Daymion, what he really needs the most is to know he is loved. You are all he has left."

Daymion bent over and gave Kayla a kiss on her forehead. She was everything a woman should be and so much more. He could see himself putting a ring on her finger and making it official. He had even purchased a six-carat diamond for the occasion, but he had been waiting for Dre to get home to share in his happiness. He also wanted to put Malachi Jensen out of his life and the only way to do that would be to kill him. Daymion was the man of the house, and it was his job to make sure his family was safe, so there would be no way he could leave his enemy walking.

Kayla smiled and hugged him tighter, but even then, she felt like it wasn't tight enough. All she wanted was for him to get past his beef with Malachi, but Daymion had been determined to avenge Kiara's death. Kayla despises the fact that even from the grave, Kiara had a hold on him, but she was damned if she'd allow her to keep it. Kiara had made her own bed and so she had to lie in it.

The quiet of the night surrounded the couple as they held each other close. From the outside looking in, one would think that it was their last embrace, but those who knew them, understood that it was their own secret language. They were so in sync with each other and could communicate without saying one word.

Kayla was worried about Daymion because he had been so obsessed with finding Malachi and making him pay for Kiara's death. It had managed to consume his every thought and had even guided his moves for years. However, no matter how insane it drove her, she was determined to stick beside him through it all. She truly loved Daymion, and not even his enemies could run her off. She just wished he would turn his focus on other things. Kayla hoped that once Dre got home, he would be an easy distraction, but what she didn't know was that Dre was even more obsessed with Malachi than his father was.

Daymion hated the fact that he was putting Kayla through the motions over some bullshit that was linked to Kiara, but she couldn't expect him to sit back and do nothing. What kind of message would that send to Dre? He believed that his son would expect nothing less than revenge on his mother's killer. Malachi had ruined everything one had ever had a hand in and had it not been for him, Kiara would have still been alive, and Dre would have never spent one day locked up. Daymion never wanted his son to experience hardship, but he knew that was how life went. Now, after spending time behind the wall, Dre would have to come home and deal with the fact that his mother was gone and was never coming back.

The sound of the doorbell broke them from their embrace. Kayla looked up at Daymion and smiled. She thought the moment he had been waiting for had finally come. The couple held hands and walked together downstairs, but when Daymion opened the door, Kayla's joy faded. She let out a disappointed sigh when she saw that it was Mellow, not because she didn't like him, but because she could tell by the look on his face that she didn't want to hear what he had to say. She shook her head and turned around so the two men could be alone.

Daymion and Mellow had met while doing time in the pen. Mellow used to be a soldier in Dory's street crew but once he got popped and was sent up the road, Dory washed his hands of him, because he only fooled with people he could use and with Mellow locked up, he was of no benefit to him. However, Mellow met Daymion Myers. Before he met him, he had heard stories about the street legend and felt like it was an honor to be in his presence. Daymion, though, only cared about what part Mellow played in Dory's crew. He was interested in finding out if the young cat had information about his son, and if he did, he wanted all of it. Daymion felt like anyone who had an affiliation with Dory, couldn't amount to a pile of shit, but Mellow surprised him and turned out to be one of the realest niggas he had ever met. The two of them became thick as thieves and had managed to remain that way.

Daymion had been scheduled to be released before Mellow, but he gave him his word that he would have a spot for him when he came home, and he stuck by every word he said. Mellow was now his right hand and did most of the footwork in the streets. Niggas knew to respect him just as much as they did Daymion, and so far, he hadn't had any problems.

"Sup, Mellow? Look like you got some shit on your mind that you need to get off."

"You damn right I do, and I can assure you it's some deep shit you gonna want to listen to."

Daymion led Mellow to the den that was downstairs. It was where they had most of their meetings, mainly because he wanted to respect Kayla's mind. He knew that she wanted no part in his street business. She felt like the less she knew, the better off she would be. Once they were inside, Daymion closed the door behind them and sat down on his black leather sofa. Mellow sat across from him in his favorite chair and lit a blunt before he told Daymion what he knew.

"My nigga, you gone need a hit of this shit when I tell you what I saw."

"Nah, I'ma pass because you know Kayla don't like that shit being smoked inside the house. However, I'ma let your ass slide this time."

"Thanks, bruh. I'ma definitely make it worth your time."

"Well, what the fuck is you waiting on? Spit that shit out."

Mellow took another pull off the blunt and then gave Daymion an update.

"The girl is back in town. People around the way say she got a crib she been staying in. even seen some nigga in and out of the place, but I ain't got no ID on him yet."

"Well then, what the hell is we waiting on? Let's go see her ass."

"Nah, Day, that shit sounds a little too easy. You don't think it's some kind of coincidence? I mean, I'm sure that bitch knows ya boy is due home. She ain't back in town for no reason. Something brought her back here. Honestly, I think we should just chill and scope shit out. We don't need to move too fast on this."

"Too fast? Nigga, I been waiting on this for years and you talking about chilling and scoping shit out. The fuck is you thinking?"

"I'm thinking about your mufuckin safety my nigga. Come on Day, you ain't new to shit like this but I think you a little too anxious. I'm one hundred with you and I think we need to strategize and come up with a game plan. I know you may not want to hear this, but we gone need Dre to fall in line with us."

"Hell no. I don't want him involved in any of this. I'm not taking that kind of risk on him, we gonna have to figure this out on our own and ain't no exceptions."

"Day, think about this for a minute, ya boy and Shay got history. We gone need him to get in the door. There's no way we can make it happen without him.

"We just gonna have to figure out a way because I ain't putting Dre in a line of fire like that."

"Why don't we let him make that decision?"

"Fuck that, I'm deciding for him. We'll find another way to get close to her, besides, we need to find out about the nigga that's been seen there. How do we know it's not Malachi?"

"Nah, they say it's a young jit but they don't know what part he plays in her life. I'll do what I can to find out.

"Look, Mell, I'ma listen and chill for a minute, at least until you can find out some more information but when I'm ready to move, I'm doing it with or without you. This shit has gone on long enough.

"Aiight, Day. Just give me some time."

Mellow sat back and took a long hard pull of the blunt and began to cough. The Kush was strong as hell, but it was the best he had smoked in a while. Since he spent most of his time out on missions, he didn't get many chances to enjoy a high. Mellow liked to have a clear mind when he would be out handling business. He was aware of the fact that not being on point could cost him his life. Living like he was living he had to always be on alert because he just never knew when shit would pop off. He swore that one day, he would pull back from the streets, but he hadn't decided when that day would come. He loved the get down too much.

Mellow truly respected Daymion, not only as a partner, but also as a friend. He hated to go against anything Daymion said but he felt that moving in on Shay too fast would end up being a death sentence for the both of them. He felt like he should scope out the scene first, because Malachi could have had killers posted up to protect his only child, and Mellow wanted to check their positions so he could be ready to strike if it came to that, and even though, Daymion was adamant about keeping Dre out of it, Mellow knew they needed him. Shit would be easier to pull off if he was there. He just hoped that Dre would go along with it. Mellow knew firsthand how Dre felt about Shay, and wondered if the feelings were still there. If they were, it could pose an even bigger problem, one that would turn father and son against one another. Mellow didn't want that to happen and hoped he could prevent it.

"Aiight, Day. I'ma get out of here and see what else I can find out, but I need you to give me your word that you won't make a move without me."

"I told you, Mell, I'ma chill. But just know, it won't be for long."

"I understand."

Mellow stood and nodded at his friend. He had hoped that Dre would show up before he left but he couldn't stick around any longer. He had to get out in the streets and make some power moves. He just prayed that he didn't make the wrong one. One that could cost him his life.

Chapter 3

Malachi Jensen sat back in his leather chair and pulled on the Cuban cigar he held between his fingers. The faint whir of the ceiling fan above him was the only sound that could be heard. He had been in his home office all morning going through stacks of bills he could no longer pay. Nobody knew it but him though, because from the outside looking in, he had his shit together. However, the truth was, the money he had amassed over his years in the drug game had quickly dwindled away.

Malachi had never been one of those dealers that invested his money because he had been too busy being flashy. He preferred recognition and random pussy over what his future could hold. He kept a nice ride, and dressed as if he was on millionaire status. He knew that was what made him stand out above the rest and it also caused the bitches to throw themselves at him. What would happen in the long run was never his concern because Malachi only lived in the here and now.

The massive home he had purchased held a nice insurance policy and caused Malachi to go to bed at night and think of ways he could cash in. He had spent a small fortune on the five thousand square foot property mainly because his daughter loved the lay out. He wanted to give her everything she desired, but lately, she had been spending less and less time there, leaving Malachi alone. The expanse had a basketball court he had never dribbled a ball on, a gym he had never worked out in and a mini theater he had never watched one movie in.

The four gunmen that were posted outside had no clue that they were on a payroll that had no more funds to pay them. Malachi thought about the lie he would tell them if they asked about what they were owed. He knew that he would only be able to put them off for so long, but before they would figure it out, he planned to be gone. Malachi had no choice but to go back out into the hoods he used to run because sitting on his ass wasn't going to put money in his pocket. He had left behind those who had been loyal to him. He left them with nothing and without an explanation, so he knew that he would be on his own.

He decided that he would let Shay think that he had gotten bored and wanted the rush that the streets gave him. She didn't need to know the truth and neither did anyone else. The last thing he wanted was for mufuckas to shame him because he was no longer on the high status he used to be on. Malachi was aware of the fact that going back out there and getting his grind on could be dangerous, but he didn't have any other choice. He had never been the type of nigga that worked for others, and he would rather die than to be someone else do boy, so he had to do things on his own. He also knew that he would be deemed vulnerable to his enemies, mainly because of his absence. Shit had changed since he'd went on hiatus so he would have to be on point and make sure that he stayed one step ahead of them at all times.

Malachi thought about why he had left town in the first place. He never really wanted to kill Kiara, because as much as he hated to admit it, he truly cared about her and had felt himself catching deeper feelings for her than he wanted. Kiara never could have replaced Malia, but she damn sure came close. When he heard that Daymion Myers had resurfaced after doing a stint in the pen, he felt like Kiara was going to leave him. She had always had a thing for him, but Malachi would rather her be six feet deep than in the next man's arms. After Kiara had done Daymion dirty, he wanted nothing else to do with her. Malachi wondered why Daymion was avenging her death so eagerly. Malachi had managed to outrun him for years but was almost certain that Daymion's mind was still on him.

The sweet sound of Shay's voice broke Malachi from his thoughts. He looked up at her in awe, the same way he used to look at Malia. Shay was just as beautiful as the woman who had given her life, and no matter how long it had been since Malia's death, the thought of her still broke his heart. He often wondered if he would ever heal and move on. Losing her had changed something inside of him, but finding out that Shay was his daughter made him want to be a better man. In all reality though, it just wasn't in him. Malachi's evil ran so deep that not even God could cleanse his soul. He knew that even as much as he loved Shay, his only child, he would kill her too if she ever sided with the enemy. So far, she had been loyal, but what Malachi didn't know was that Shay had a thing for the enemy's son.

"Hey, what are you doing in here all by yourself?"

"Just sorting through some papers and planning some things. Got some stuff I'd like to get out and do."

"Really? What kind of stuff are you talking about?"

"Honestly, I was thinking about going back to where I started and getting my grind on again. It's starting to get a little boring here by myself. I mean, you don't ever stick around anymore. Plus, I kinda miss the excitement and the power the streets gave me. How do you feel about that?"

"I'm not sure how I feel. Maybe you should be asking Daymion Myers that question instead of me."

"And just what in the hell do you mean by that?"

"I'm just saying dad, what if he's still out there waiting for you to show your face? It still feels like yesterday that you came into my life and I'm not ready to lose you."

"I'm not worried about Daymion, and you shouldn't be either. When and if he finds out I'm back in town and he comes at me, I'll be ready."

Shay walked around her father's cherry wood desk, stood in front of him and crossed her arms over her chest. He could see her biting the inside of her cheek, a move she made when she was nervous and was about to say something he wouldn't like. He waited with hidden anticipation until she finally spoke.

"I'm moving back. Actually, I've already done it. I've wanted to tell you for a few weeks now, but I just didn't know how, but since you're talking about going back, I figured it was a perfect time."

"So, I guess that tells me why you haven't been home as much, but what the hell were you thinking? You know that mufucka is probably still waiting for me to show my face. What if he would have seen you and done something to you because of me? That bastard is the one that put a bullet through your mother's throat. You don't think he will do the same to you?"

"He won't. Daymion Myers would never hurt me, so you don't need to worry."

"The fuck you mean don't worry? You're a part of me, just like your mother was. He won't spare you Monshay. He will use you to get to me."

"I'm telling you, dad, he's not going to hurt me. From what I understand, he didn't intentionally kill my mother. He was aiming at Dory, but Dory pulled my mother in front of him. That bastard used her as a shield. Dory knew that bullet was meant for him, and you knew it too."

"And yet, you laid up under his ass like shit was sweet. As if he wasn't the reason she's gone. You totally disrespected her name, and I don't know, maybe I'm missing something here because you sure seem to know a whole hell of a lot about Daymion Myers."

"I don't know shit about him. I just did my homework and found out what I wanted to know. If he would have killed her intentionally, you wouldn't have to be worried about him right now because I would have killed him myself, but he didn't. Daymion Myers was never your enemy, or hers."

Malachi scrunched his eyebrows together and took a second before he leaned forward and put his cigar that had long before gone out, in the ashtray. He uncrossed his legs and stood, towering over Shay. when she looked up at him, he could tell that she was nervous, and she had every right to be.

"How dare you stand before me and defend him as if he's done nothing wrong. He killed the only woman I have ever gave a damn about and that shit done something to me. My heart ain't never been the same."

"I'm sorry you feel like that, but I am not defending him. I'm just tired of you sitting around here worrying about him. My mother's death affected me too, but I can't spend all my time dwelling on it. Look at you dad, you can't even live your life because you don't know what corner he is creeping around, and yet you tell me that you're ready to get back out there and grind. I meant what I said. You should ask Daymion how he feels about it because he's the only one that has been stopping you. I think you two need to squash that dumb shit and call a truce. He killed my mother, and you killed his son's mother. No matter how much more blood gets shed nothing will change that. Call it even and move the hell on."

Malachi couldn't believe what Shay had said. What she was asking of him was impossible… There could never be peace between him and Daymion. The damage had already been done and it was too deep to cover it up and walk away. The only option he had was to go out there and make his presence known and once Daymion Myers figured it out, Malachi would be ready to lay him down.

Chapter 4

"Yo, I got one more spot I need you to take me to before we go to my pops' place."

"Uh-uh Dre. hell no. Your father gave me specific instructions to follow and I've already gone against them once. I'm not doing it again."

"Well, at least I know whose side you would be on if me and him were to ever go to war with each other. That's why you could never be my bitch, because my bitch wouldn't give a fuck what the next man said, no matter who that man was. She would honor my word because to her, my word would be bond. Shit, you got some damn nerve to throw salt at Shay when your ass ain't got no loyalty either."

The words cut through Tasha like a freshly sharpened blade. She couldn't remember Dre ever being that cruel to her, but it seemed as if doing time hardened him. She hated the fact that he had compared her to Shay because she was nothing like her and never would be. She hoped in time, he would realize that too, because nothing meant more to her than him.

"I'm nothing like her, Dre. I'm the one that's been loyal to you from day one and you know that. I went against my own brother for you. So, what you talking ain't shit. Your father has been good to me, and he trusts me. I never want to lose his respect, and I don't want to give him any reason to ban me from your life."

"The fuck you mean? The only one who can ban you from me and my life, is me. We grown now, Tasha, so fucking act like it."

Dre watched as her nose flared in anger while the tears formed in her eyes. He had hurt her and he knew it. She had been so used to the softer side of him, but he wasn't that person anymore. The sooner she realized that, the better off she would be. He cared deeply for Tasha, but he needed a bitch on his team that would stand up for him. Fuck what the next man said.

"Well then, I guess I better enjoy what I have now because as soon as you reconnect with Shay, you won't need me anymore."

"I'll always need you, Tasha, but I gotta know that you gone ride for me, not another nigga."

"Yeah, you say you need me, but I'm not going to keep being your duck while you smelling that bitch. She never did a damn thing for you except fuck you over and yet your black ass is still running behind her as if she's been an innocent bystander in all of this. Shay has Malachi Jensen's blood pumping through her veins, and everybody knows that his DNA is full of poison. The only thing she can do for you is put you in harm's way, and damn it Dre, I am not about to let that happen. I'll swallow that bullet before I let it get to you."

Dre was at a loss for words at the revelation that Tasha would be willing to die just to protect him. He had always known that she felt some type of way for him, but he never could have imagined such a sacrifice. Deep down he knew that Shay would not be willing to do the same, but still, he wasn't ready to fully let her go. He also wasn't about to walk away from Tasha either. She had been there for him in ways that no one else had and he believed that she always would be.

"So, you willing to die to save a nigga, but you won't do what I ask. Type of shit is that?"

"That's some real type of shit. That's something Shay will never give you. Now, where in the hell am I taking you?"

Dre smiled and shook his head and then gave Tasha directions. He had to admit, she was giving him a run for his money, but he knew it would be well worth it in the end. He needed Tasha more than she knew because she could be trusted. She had proven it more than once, and if he lived long enough to be the king of the streets, he would need someone like her beside him. They didn't make thoroughbreds like her anymore and he knew that.

When she pulled up to the house that he had led her to, Dre let out a sigh of relief. Other than the high grass that surrounded the property, it still looked the same. He just hoped that what he went there for was still in the place that he had left it. Tasha sat there and wondered what Dre would do next because he either had the wrong address or he was losing his mind.

"Are you sure that this is the right place? I mean, it looks like no one lives here anymore. Maybe we should just go."

"Nah, it's correct. Just chill for a minute. I'ma get out and go around back so I can get what I came for. I won't be long."

"Okay, I'ma wait, but I'm keeping the car running. I mean, this place looks real spooky so I'm not taking any chances and if I see anything move wrong, I'm shooting."

"What? There ain't gone be no need for all that. Besides, what the hell you doing with a gun?"

"Dre, I've had a gun since I was fourteen. Remember, it was me who killed Malice, because my pussy ass brother couldn't pull the trigger."

"Yeah, I remember, but I need you to sit back and chill. Let me go get what I came for and then we can leave."

"Alright, but hurry up."

Tasha locked the doors as soon as Dre got out. She had never been a scary bitch, but the house had her creeped out. Something about it was off, she just couldn't figure out what it was. She picked up the gun she had sitting in her lap and checked it. She had to make sure it was ready, just in case she had to bust a cap in somebody's ass.

Dre treaded carefully though the high grass, because he wasn't sure what was hiding in it. He felt like he was tough enough, but if he encountered a snake, he was going to run like a pussy and didn't care what anyone said. He didn't fuck around when it came to snakes, especially the humankind. When he made it safely to the back of the house, he looked around to make sure he was still alone and then he continued his trek until he got to the bush he had buried his treasure beside. It was dark out, but the moon provided just enough light for him to see that what he had worked so hard for was gone.

Dre hung his head and closed his eyes. He thought he had been careful every time he pushed his money into the box he had concealed in the earth, but someone must have seen him because the earth had been opened up and jacked. He couldn't remember exactly how much had been in that stash, but he knew it was enough to get him on his feet. Now, he would have to crawl until he could walk again. He never could understand why shit never worked in his favor. From the time he had taken his first breath, he had been doomed and to that day, he never understood why.

The voice that came from behind was one that was familiar, but he remembered it being a little more mature. Still, there was no mistaken git. Dre suddenly wished that he had brought along Tasha's piece, but since he hadn't, he hoped things wouldn't lead to gun play. If it did, Dre was truly fucked.

"You ain't gotta waste your time looking for that stash, playa. Shit been gone. It disappeared as soon as your ass got booked."

Dre turned around slowly with his hands up and faced his one-time friend. The night sky illuminated Kenny's face just enough for Dre to see the evil it possessed. He couldn't recall why Kenny had become the opps. He wondered if the truth had been there all along and if so, how did he miss it?

"You took my shit, Kenny? I worked my ass off for that change and you know it. The fuck did you become my enemy?"

"From day one, mufucka. Ain't no friends out here in these streets. It's each man for theyself. You know that."

"Nigga, you can eat that shit you talking because I pulled you in on everything that came at me. Don't be mad because you was too pussy to handle it."

"Pussy, huh? They should have gave your ass life because everything you left behind belongs to me now. Including your bitch."

"Fuck is you talking about?"

"I'm talking about Shay pretty ass, nigga. That ho jumped on my dick hard as soon as those cuffs were secured around your wrists. Bitch sucks my shit every night."

Dre could not believe what Kenny had said to him. He felt like the nigga was lying because there was no way Shay would do something so low, at least that's what he thought. He had to remember though, Shay had turned out to be shady so anything was possible, but Dre had to act like it didn't bother him in the least.

"Man, I don't give a damn about what Shay does. That bitch left me for dead and she gone do the same thing to you. Watch and see what I tell you."

"Nah, I got Shay right where I want her and ain't shit you can do to change that."

"Okay. So now what? You got my money, and you got my bitch, but guess what, nigga. Even if you take my life, you still could never be me."

"Be you? That's some funny shit because last time I checked, you was a nobody. You ain't even a memory to the mufuckas out here. Your own momma ain't even give a damn about you. And ya daddy? That fuck nigga ain't shit. He a pussy, just like you."

"A pussy, huh? You got some nerve. You couldn't even pull the trigger on a nigga that violated your fam, and yet, here you are acting like you run some shit. Know this nigga, you ain't gonna ever run a damn thing, whether I'm dead or alive."

"Well, I guess we just gone have to see about that, ain't we?"

Dre wanted to run up on Kenny and fuck him up, but he wasn't sure if his rival had a weapon or not. If he did, he didn't want to take the chance of him using it before he could get him down. The two of them stood and stared at each other for a moment and right when Kenny was about to say something else he heard movement coming from the side of the house. Kenny wasn't about to hang around and see who it was, so he took one last look at Dre and took off through the woods. No sooner than he was out of sight, Tasha appeared.

"Dre? Is that you? What the hell is taking you so long? This place has me really creeped out and I'm not about to keep sitting out there by myself. Are you ready to go yet?"

"Yeah, Tasha, I'm ready."

When Dre got closer to her, she noticed that he didn't have anything in his hands and gave him a sideways look. She could have sworn that he told her he was there to pick something up so she couldn't understand why he was still empty handed.

"I thought you said you had to pick something up. Where is it at?"

"It's not here anymore, Tasha."

"What you mean, it's not here anymore? Where is it? Don't tell me we got to stop somewhere else."

"My money. It's gone. I used to bury all my money back here so my mom wouldn't take it, but it's gone. Someone beat me to it."

"So, what are you gonna do now?"

"I'ma get out there on my grind and stack back up. What else am I supposed to do?"

"Dre, you do know that your father is a millionaire, don't you? I'm sure he can triple what you lost. All without you having to put in any work."

"I'm not about to depend on the next man for a come up. Not even my father. Hell, I came this far without him, and I learned years ago that when other mufuckas cover you, it's for their benefit only. I got me, so don't you worry about it."

Tasha shrugged and turned around. She didn't have time to just stand there and deal with Dre's stubbornness. She just wanted to get the hell out of there. Dre shook his head and followed behind her, still trying to believe that Kenny got him for his stash. That was his second strike and his last. Dre would not give him any more chances.

Once he was in the car with Tasha, he decided to question her so he could find out just how much she knew about her brother. Dre needed to make sure that he wasn't headed for a set up. True enough, Tasha treaded through the mud with him, but he still felt like he should be cautious. No matter what anyone said, blood was still thicker than water.

"Aye, when you said was the last time you saw your brother?"

"Kenny? I haven't seen Kenny since the night you got arrested."

"You sure about that?"

"Hold up, Dre, what the hell are you implying? You know I don't fuck with him like that. I never even forgave him for betraying you."

"I'm just saying, Tasha. That's your blood, and no matter what you spittin', blood has always been thicker than water."

"Yeah. Well, Kenny's veins don't pump blood. They pump oil, and we all know that oil and water don't mix."

"Well, for your sake, let's hope you right."

Chapter 5

Mellow sat back in his box Chevy and bobbed his head to the sounds of Bryann T as he rapped about being "Free and Forgiven". He could only listen to the Christian rapper when he was alone because he felt like other mufuckas would look at him sideways. No one knew it, but Mellow had been raised in the church and had managed to always keep a hold of his faith. He decided to keep his religious upbringing hidden from the niggas on the block because he felt like they would look at him as being weak and possibly even try him.

Living life on both sides of the fence was hard at times because no matter how much Mellow tried to follow the commandments God had set forth, he broke them on a daily basis. He knew that Christians weren't supposed to take lives or harm others, but he had done his share of sending people to their final resting place. Not only by the gun, but also by the poison he pushed out in the streets. He swore to himself and to God that one day, he would lay it all down and surrender. He just wasn't sure when that day would come.

"Haters hatin' for no reason. Throwing salt, they forget I was seasoned."

Mellow had been rapping along with Bryann T, word for word when he saw movement from the corner of his eye. He quickly sat up, shut the music off and focused his attention on the figure that was at the front door of the place he had been watching. It wasn't a female, so he figured it was the nigga that had been seen frequenting the spot. He picked his cell up from the passenger seat and began to dial Daymion's number but changed his mind before all the digits were in. He wanted to find out who the nigga was and what was going on with him before reaching out. Daymion was ready to make moves without having any information and Mellow thought it was a bad idea. He wanted to know just what they would be stepping into first.

Once dude was inside, Mellow checked his weapon to make sure it was ready and then quietly stepped out of his ride. He crept up to the side of the house and peeked in a window. The gap in the curtains was small so he wasn't able to get a good sighting, but he felt like the nigga was alone. Instead of going back to the front, Mellow crept around to the back door. He had learned how to pick locks at a young age because his cousin felt like he needed to know how to get out of doors that he didn't want to be locked behind.

Mellow pushed the straight pin into the key slot and after a couple of pokes and swipes, the door unlocked with ease. Once he made sure his weapon was handy and ready to shoot, he slowly turned the knob and pushed the door open. After checking to make certain no one was behind it, Mellow walked in. The strong stench of crack being smoked hit his senses immediately. Mellow had been in plenty of crack houses looking for mufuckas that owed him so he could pick up on the drug's scent anywhere.

The smell became stronger as he walked further into the house. Finally, the flame from a lighter came into view. Mellow stopped and stood silent for a minute so he could calculate his next move. He hoped to try and get a good look at the nigga to see if he recognized him, but the flame coming from the lighter, revealed nothing new. Mellow waited for the room to go dark and cocked his weapon.

"Hey. Somebody there? Who is that? I ain't got no damn money so you wasting your time. You might as well just go ahead and leave."

The nigga struck the lighter again when he got no response, only to find the barrel of a gun looking back at him. His hand began to tremble in fear of what he thought was to come. He shook so badly, the flame ended up burning his thumb and it caused him to drop the lighter.

"Come on, Mane. Stop playing fucking games. I ain't got a damn thing to give you."

Mellow finally spoke in the darkness.

"Actually, I think you may have everything I'm looking for."

"Wha-What do you mean? What the hell do you want?"

"Where is the young lady that's been coming here with you? And don't try to lie because if you do, you'll never strike another lighter again."

"Dammit, I knew that bitch was going to get me hemmed up in some bullshit. She ain't here, though. She left out earlier, said she had to pay someone a visit."

"Who did she go to see? Did she mention that part?"

"Nah, she ain't tell me all that. We have a mutual agreement. I don't ask no questions and she don't volunteer no information. It just works better for us that way, and that's the God's honest truth."

"The truth huh? I tell you what. Why don't you let me decide if it's the truth or not? Go head and get up really slow and turn on a light in here. I need to look in your eyes when you talk to me so I can make my own determination. Don't try no funny shit though, because if you do, you gone be shitting in a bag for the rest of your life."

Deep down, Mellow believed that the nigga was telling the truth, but he couldn't walk away and let him off the hook that easy, plus, he wanted to see who he had run up on in hopes of gaining a better grip on what he had to get done. He knew that Daymion wouldn't wait long before he would be ready to make a move so Mellow had to be sure his shit was accurate. He couldn't let his friend walk into a bullshit situation and risk his life.

Mellow backed up with his gun still pointed out in front of him. He prayed that the nigga wans't dumb enough to try no stupid shit because he hadn't went there with the intention to kill someone, but to save his own skin, he would do it in a minute.

When the light finally clicked on, Mellow took a good long look at the nigga. He felt like he knew him from somewhere, but his memory betrayed him. He wondered if the mufucka felt the same way, but by the look on his face, Mellow didn't think so.

"Nigga, I know you from somewhere. What they call you? Refresh me."

"Look, mane, you don't know me and I don't want no trouble but if you put that gun down, I might be able to think a little clearer and help you out."

"So, you trying to make the rules now? It don't work like that. Now you gonna think clearly and help me out whether I put this gun down or not."

"Man, fuck you. I ain't doing shit. You just gonna have to kill me."

"Alright, your choice."

Mellow couldn't believe the nigga was testing him. That crack must have had him thinking he was untouchable or something, but little did he know, he was going to be touched if he didn't start talking. Mellow hadn't went there to waste his time on bullshit and he wasn't leaving without something he could use. He decided to test the nigga's gangsta and find out just how tough he really was. He had broke many mufuckas and there would be no exception.

Mellow ran up on him before he had a chance to move and busted him in the head with the butt of his weapon. When the mufucka fell to his knees, Mellow pushed the barrel of the gun to his temple and once he felt like he got the message, he spoke again.

"See, now that's where ya wrong. You gonna do everything I tell you, and you gone start by picking your pretty little girlfriend's brain. Find out where her father is hiding out and report that information back to me. In return, I'ma let you continue to breathe. It's him I want but if you're willing to risk your life for his, then so be it."

"Look, she ain't never talked about her father around me, only her mother. Let's say she don't tell me shit. Then what?"

"Then you make her, or you will find out how cold steel tastes in your mouth. I don't give a damn how you get the information. Just get it, now have a good night."

"Wait. How do I find you once I get it?"

"You don't. You wait for me to come to you."

Mellow walked out and left the man on his knees without another word. He was sure that the nigga would do what he had to do to gain the information because most mufuckas cared more about their own life than someone else's. Mellow hoped it didn't come to gunplay because he felt like he couldn't afford to commit another sin. God may have forgiven him for many but eventually they were going to lead him straight to hell.

"Who told you gangsters go to heaven? Who told you money makes you real? Who told you pistols make you tough? You don't see all the dead bodies on the field?"

The words from Bryann T. filled Mellows mental once again and made him rethink what he had just done. It was too late to turn back but he swore that after he helped Daymion find Malachi, he would hang up his gangsta boots and walk with the Lord, he only hoped he lived long enough to do it.

Chapter 6

Daymion rushed to the front door like a mad man as soon as he heard the vehicle pull up in his driveway. He was pissed and had been pacing the floor for hours. He was good and ready to give Tasha a piece of his mind. He had trusted her to follow his instructions, and she had let him down. He deposed disobedient people, no matter who they were. Kayla had tried her best to calm him, but she was fruitless, because when Daymion told someone to do something he expected them to follow through. Those who didn't usually got dealt with and he would show no favor when it came to Tasha. She needed to understand that he was not a man to go against.

"Where in the hell have you been at? I told you exactly what you needed to do, and you obviously went against everything I said. I thought that I could trust you with one little task and you fucked me. It's good to know that I can't depend on you, and I don't appreciate that shit one bit. And where the hell is my son anyway?"

Dre suddenly appeared behind Tasha and gently pushed her to the side. He wasn't happy with the way his father talked to her and felt like he should let him know it. Dre was a man now and wanted the respect he deserved, along with anyone who rode beside him, and one way or the other, he was going to get it.

"You need to watch how you speak to my bitch. You also need to know that your rules no longer apply when it comes to her. She follows what I say now. You might as well get used to it."

"Your bitch huh? That's what a woman is to you? So, I guess that's what they taught you on the inside."

"Someone had to teach me something. Shit, I'd say it's more than you ever did."

The words hit Daymion like a hard kick to the stomach and nearly took his breath away. He wondered if Dre had picked up the bad boy attitude from being locked up, or was he like that because of Daymion's absence when he was growing up. Whichever one it was, he would not stand for the disrespect in his house, even if it was coming from his own blood!

"How dare you come at me like that when you know that I had no say so in that situation. Now this is supposed to be a happy time for us, please don't ruin it."

Kayla heard the pain in Daymion's voice and rushed to his side to save the day, which was what she usually did. She hoped to be able to stop any drama before it unfolded. Daymion had waited so long to finally have Dre in his life, and she didn't want to see him suffer another setback. Something would have to give, one way or another.

"Dre. We are so glad you're finally home. We have been waiting for this day for so long, so please, let's not start it like this. You and your father have so much to catch up on. Don't ruin it."

Dre's demeanor softened at the sound of Kayla's voice. She always seemed to have a way of calming him down and making him feel better. Maybe it was because he knew beyond a shadow of a doubt that she truly cared about him and his wellbeing. She had always been more of a mother to him than his own and he never wanted to disappoint her. He had already been through so much shit, and he knew that there was no need to conger up anymore. Dre would try to keep peace, at least for the time being.

"You know what? You right, auntie Kayla. Me and my pops got a lot of shit we need to sort through. Things we need to catch up on and it's gone happen, but it's gonna have to wait until another time. I got more important things to handle right now. We can do all that bonding shit when I'm done taking care of my business."

Daymion knew that Dre was talking about Malachi, but he didn't want his son going after the bastard. He knew that he should have handled it before Dre came home but he had given up the search, hoping that Malachi would come out on his own, but his hopes had been shattered because the nigga had yet to show his face.

"Dre, I don't want you to worry about Malachi. He's going to be taken care of and when he does, I want your hands to be clean. I'll make sure the job gets done."

"Yeah? Well that sounds good, but I been gone four long ass years and you ain't shook that nigga yet. I'm having a hard time understanding what the problem is."

"Malachi has been in hiding and I haven't been able to get a grip on him yet. I will though, and that's my word."

"Your word is something I don't need because it seems like you ain't living by it. That bastard was supposed to be dealt with before my momma was covered in dirt. Here it is, all these years later and he's still walking around breathing."

"I know that you may think it's easy to take a mufucka out but it's not. The time and place have to match up and it hasn't. That coward disappeared with his daughter and hasn't been seen since. I'm going to get him Dre. I just need you to pull back and stay out of the way so I can handle it. I wouldn't be able to live with myself if something happened to you."

Dre stared into Daymion's eyes and could tell that he was being genuine. He was aware of all the shit his mother had done to keep him and his father apart, and because of that, he felt like he should cut him some slack. However, he was not about to sit back while Daymion went into a war that he shouldn't fight alone. Malachi was Dre's enemy too and he wanted the pleasure of taking his life. He couldn't let his father get all the glory.

"Stepping back is something I'm not going to do. That was my fucking mother he took, and he had no right. I fight that battle with you, or I go on my own your choice pops."

Daymion knew that he wouldn't be able to change Dre's mind no matter how much he tried. The last thing he wanted was for his only heir to go into a war and not make it out, but he couldn't stop him. Dre wasn't that same innocent seventeen-year-old boy who he had met in visitation that day. He had grown up and into a man that mirrored Daymion's own image. He understood the need to let Dre fight and the only thing he could do was fight with him and get it done.

"Aiight, Dre. I understand your position, but you have to agree that you don't move without me. We fight that nigga together."

"It's a deal, but you have to do the same."

Before Daymion could say another word, Mellow walked in. He was about to speak but noticed Dre and stopped. The young nigga had grown up, but his identity couldn't be mistaken. He smiled and pulled Dre in for a hug. Mellow could feel the hesitation from him but he refused to pull back. Dre was like family to him and no amount of time could change that. When he finally let him go, he looked around the room to all who were present. He acknowledged Kayla and Tasha before he turned his attention back on Dre.

"Sup, Dre? Glad to have you back home. I see you done grew up and shit."

"Yeah, it's good to be out of that hell hole. Damn sure don't wanna go through that again. And I apologize for being a little hesitant at first. It's just been a while. What's going on with you, though?"

"Just been chilling, that's all. Just came by to holla at your pops and if it's okay with him, you more than welcome to join. Might be some shit you wanna hear anyway."

Mellow looked at Daymion just to make sure that he hadn't overstepped his boundaries and when he nodded, Mellow knew that it was all good. He had honestly forgotten about Dre coming home after his encounter with the nigga from earlier that night. He couldn't believe that he didn't even get his name, but it actually didn't matter because he would remember his face.

Mellow hated to intrude on Daymion and Dre's time together, but what he had to say couldn't wait. He turned and smiled at Kayla who nodded and then walked out of the room with Tasha on her heels. She could tell that Tasha was still bothered by Daymion's harsh words but she knew that in the end, all would be forgiven. Daymion truly admired Tasha because he knew her feelings for Dre were one hundred. He just hoped Dre's were the same.

Once the three men were alone, Daymion was the first to speak. He wanted Mellow to know that he had agreed with including Dre.

"Feel free to say what you need to say, Mellow. Dre gone ride with us. It's his right."

"Aiight, then. I was sitting on the house that I saw Shay, and that nigga showed up."

Dre sat up straight at the mention of Shay's name. He wondered what house Mellow had mentioned and how long she had been there. He knew that he should shake her, but until he got some answers, there was no way that he could.

"That nigga you talking about is Kenny. He's Tasha's brother. We used to be tight until his ass turned on me, but I'ma get in his ass for the old and the new. Mufucka dug up my stash and he's gonna have to make up for that. And Shay, he can have her ass. I don't need a grimygrimy hoe like that in my life anyway."

Mellow remembered the first time Dre had laid eyes on Shay. he saw the attraction from the jump and knew it wouldn't be a good thing. Not only because she was Dory's girl, but also because she didn't know how to be loyal. He had wanted to warn Dre but never got a chance to do it. Shay had always been a grimy bitch, just like her mother. Mellow was surprised that she had ended up with Dre's partner. That was just the type of hoe she was.

"I knew that nigga looked familiar, but I just couldn't place him. That mufucka used to run with Malice before he got killed. I walked up on him hitting the pipe. Shit got his ass unrecognizable, scared the hell out of him, but still ain't got no information. He claimed that Shay don't tell him anything and I hate to say it, but I believe him. Told him to find out about her father if he wanted to live."

Daymion paid close attention to Dre's reaction to what he had heard. At first, when Mellow had mentioned using Dre to lure Shay in, Daymion wasn't down with it, but he now realized that Dre would be the only way in.

He wondered if Shay would fall for it and also, if Dre's feelings for her would make a difference in the plan. Pussy made men weak, and he just hoped that Dre would be the exception.

"Look, son, we need you to get close to Shay so we can get close to Malachi, but you got to be sure you don't get caught up."

"Nah, pops, that ain't gonna happen because those feelings have been gone. I can do it, but I got to get rid of Kenny first. He's gonna be a problem if I don't."

"Okay, how you want to handle that? You want me to send somebody in to do the job?"

"Hell nah, that nigga is mine and mine only. I'ma teach his ass how to keep his hands off of other people's property, but let me get my mind right first, 'cause when I shoot, I gotta make sure I don't miss."

Chapter 7

After spending some time catching up with his father and Kayla, Dre decided that it was best if he stayed in a hotel, at least for the time being. He hated to disappoint them but adjusting to freedom had not been as easy as he thought it would be. Dre had so much shit going on his mind and needed to deal with it before he pressed on. He hadn't even been out for twenty-four hours and was already faced with drama. The shit going on between Kenny and Shay had him vexed. He couldn't believe that Shay would go out like that because he had her pegged as a different type of female than any other he had met. She had ended up being just as grimy as the next bitch, though, and he couldn't wait to set her ass straight.

Dre took a moment and glanced over at Tasha who had mostly been quiet ever since Daymion went off on her. He knew that she had grown close to his father, and it had hurt her for him to talk to her that way. That was why Dre felt the need to straighten him. He wondered if he had offended her by referring to her as his bitch. She had to know that it was just a figure of speech, and he meant no disrespect behind it. Tasha had proven herself three times over. Dre knew that no matter what happened, she would always be the one he could turn to. He often wondered why she cared so much about him when he had never given her a reason. He knew there was only one way to find out.

"Aye, Tasha. Why you so stuck on a nigga? I ain't neva did shit to make you feel special, and yet, you still around while other mufuckas dipped on me. What's your motive?"

"My motive, Dre, is to show you your worth. You been through enough already. Somebody has to give a damn about you. Why can't it be me?"

"I'm just saying. Am I really worth all the bullshit you've gone through? You lost your fam behind it, and honestly, your life, because you could be somewhere with a good man but you here with me."

"That's because it's where I want to be. You it for me, Dre, and if our bodies never meet, I still won't give myself to anyone else. That's my word."

Dre didn't doubt what Tasha had said because she had never given him reason to. He smiled and then laid his seat back. When thoughts of Shay came to his mind he did his best to suppress them but they just wouldn't go away. She was supposed to be his future queen, but her true colors shined and left a sour taste in his mouth. He wasn't sure yet how he was going to react once he saw her again. Her presence alone used to make him weak in the knees, but he was certain that he would now stand strong. He had made plans to go with Mellow that weekend to sit outside the house she was seen at. They were hopeful that she would show up. Dre already knew that Kenny was going to be a problem, but he wasn't going to let that stop him.

Dre felt the car come to a stop and noticed that Tasha had pulled into the Ramada. He let his seat up and wondered why she was just sitting there instead of getting out. Hell, he was ready to relax from the long day he had. Too much had already went on in such a short time and he just needed a release.

"Why you just sitting there like a statue? The room ain't gonna get itself."

"Because I know that once I go get this room key, you'll send me on my way and I'm not ready to leave you yet. I just want a little more time."

"Nah, Tasha, you got it all mixed up. I want you to get a room for us, not me. I want you to be in there with me. You really think I'ma let your ass go? You got me fucked up if you do."

"You say that, but what about Shay? I overheard the conversation at your father's house, so I know you are going to her. What's going to happen after that, Dre?"

"Ain't shit gone happen, so chill. I'm just doing what I need to do to get to that mufucka that took my momma out. I'ma need her in order to get to him, but right now, this shit is all about me and you. Let's keep it that way."

Tasha nodded even though she still felt like she would lose in the end. She decided to make the best of what she could while she was with him. Dre let out a long sigh when she finally got out of the car. She was only gone a few minutes before she came back with the room key dangling from her fingers. Dre could tell from the look on her face that she wasn't sure of what would happen, but he would do everything in his power to take away all her doubts. She was nervous and little did she know, he was nervous too.

Dre got out and when he slammed the door shut, Tasha jumped. He shook his head and laughed at her innocence. He couldn't believe that he never noticed how beautiful she really was. He wondered how he could have missed it. Dre gently grabbed Tasha by the hand and together, they walked to the room.

Once they got inside and shut the door behind them, Dre wasted no time. He pulled Tasha into his arms and pressed his lips against hers with passion he didn't know he had inside of him. When their kiss finally broke, they locked eyes and stared at one another, both with a look of fear. Tasha felt her heart speed up and put her hand over it as if she could slow it down. She had been patient and had waited so long for that day to happen, and now that it was there, she had no clue what to do with it.

"Dre. Um. What was that for?"

"It was to show you that shit is real with me. You keep questioning me, and I felt like you needed that answer. I'm ready to go all in, Tasha, but I ain't gone lie, you gonna have to lead the way. A nigga like me ain't never did this before."

Tasha was shocked at the words Dre had spoken. She always thought that him and Shay had went all the way together, but to find out different, made her believe in him so much more. It gave her more courage and self-confidence. She felt like she could actually be it for him, but she didn't have experience either. The only male that had ever touched her was Malice, and it was by force. She hated that it had happened, but she often thought about the baby it had produced. She had been mad at God for taking it from her but realized that it wasn't supposed to happen with him, but with someone she truly loved, like Dre.

"Are you being honest with me, Dre, or you just trying to impress me so I'll give it up? I mean, I thought you and Shay went all the way with each other."

"Nah, it never came to that. Now that I think about it, I'm glad it never did. There's no one I would rather share this with than you."

Tasha smiled and wrapped her arms around Dre's neck so she could get a good grip on him before she kissed him again. Her hold on him was tight, but he refused to let her loosen it. Without breaking the embrace, Dre put his hands on her waist and walked her one step at a time to the bed. Only then did their kiss get interrupted.

The buzzing of Tasha's cell phone brought their rendezvous to an end. She didn't want to even look and see who the caller was because she felt like she already knew. She had even decided to hold off buying him a cell phone until the day after he got out. She felt like it would only be a distraction, and she wanted to spend a little time with him first when her cell buzzed again, Dre shook his head and told her not to answer it, but Tasha had already been scolded by Daymion once and she couldn't afford another fuck up no matter what Dre said. It was Daymion who had held her down while Dre was locked up. Tasha had went from hood status to super stardom overnight.

Dre didn't know it yet, but Tasha was one of Daymion's top soldiers. She sold more dope and brought in more money than half the niggas on his payroll, and she wasn't trying to slow down. She liked the fact that she never had to wait on hand outs because she had her own shit. Her rose gold Benz and Black card were small things compared to the four-bedroom house she owned in a small cul-de-sac surrounded by white people. She hoped to take Dre there, but she didn't want to put too much on him too soon. Tasha knew that he was going to be pissed when he found out that she was dealing for his father. However, she wanted to make sure she was the one to tell him, she just didn't know how she was going to do it yet.

"Dre, I have to answer the call. It's your father and he's probably calling for you anyway."

Tasha didn't wait for a response. She pressed her lips together and answered. Sure enough, it was Daymion, and he wanted to talk to Dre, not her, so she passed him the phone and without another word, walked off and into the bathroom so he could have some privacy. She didn't know why, but she had a bad feeling in the pit of her stomach about the call, and not even three minutes later, she heard a light knock at the bathroom door. When she opened it, she could tell from the look on his face that what had started between them was already over.

Tasha walked out of the bathroom and picked her car keys up from the table. She turned and stole one last look at Dre and then opened the room door. She didn't want to hear anything he had to say because she didn't think she would like it. Tasha was ready to take him where he needed to go because she was ready to cry and didn't want him to see her do it.

"Nah, ma. You can just chill here and wait for me. Mellow is on his way to get me. I ain't gonna be long. Just going to check some shit out."

The thought of Dre coming back to her made Tasha feel a little better about the situation, but in the back of her mind, she wondered what would happen if he ran into Shay. She still couldn't shake the thoughts of Dre and Shay being together. Tasha had so many what ifs on the tip of her tongue but she just wasn't brave enough to ask them. When Dre walked up behind her and put his arms around her slim waist, she jumped as if he had spooked her but then she closed the door back and shut her eyes. Her moment had finally come and once again Shay had fucked it up, at least, that was how she felt. However, she would try to keep those feelings to herself.

"Okay, Dre I'll stay and wait for you. I mean, done already waited four years. What's a couple of more hours?"

As soon as Tasha turned to face him, a light knock sounded at the door. Dre bent down to kiss her, but she wasn't feeling it anymore, so she turned her head. That phone call had crushed her spirit and all she wanted at that moment was to be alone so she could get herself together. She freed herself from his hold and stepped away and when the door slammed from behind her, she breathed a sigh of relief. Suddenly, she had the urge to run out of the door behind him and try to stop what he was about to do. Tasha felt like she should have tried to talk him out of leaving, but it was too late. Dre was gone, with a promise that he would be back. She wasn't sure if she believed him, though.

Tasha decided to sit on the edge of the bed and try to wait it out. Hopefully, she wouldn't have to wait long, if she did, she planned to tell him to kiss her ass. She didn't deserve to be put on hold for the next bitch. Tasha knew her worth and if Dre couldn't see that by now, it would be his loss because her days of waiting for him were over.

Chapter 8

The darkness of the window kept Dre hidden from view, but for some reason, he felt like he could still be seen. He reached down and pulled the lever on the side of the seat and leaned back but made sure he was still high enough to see out. He was glad that his father trusted Mellow enough to pick him up alone. Daymion would have wanted to ask a lot of questions and Dre wasn't really up for giving answers. He already knew Tasha would be in his ear as soon as he went back to the room and honestly, he would rather deal with her than Daymion.

It was late, but there were still plenty of dealers out on the corner. Some of them Dre remembered from before, but others were complete strangers. He never really fucked with a lot of people when he was out, and he preferred to keep it that way. He thought back to when he had pushed that poison out on the block. It had never been his dream, so he wasn't the best at it, but he had been good enough to accumulate a nice little paper stash from it. The same stash that Kenny had claimed to take from him. Dre was vexed about how the nigga knew where his spot was in the first place, because he had been very careful not to ever be followed there. It was too late to worry about it though, because his shit was gone and if what Mellow said about Kenny was true, it had already been smoked up.

Dre sat his seat up a little when he felt the ride slow down. He noticed that Mellow had turned down a side street he was unfamiliar with. Dre had been all over the block before and wasn't sure how he had missed that one particular road. He looked from side to side but didn't recognize anything. Dre wasn't impressed by the expensive rides parked in front of the even more expensive houses that lined the block. That type of material shit had never done much for him. He had always been low key and wasn't about to change up.

Dre paid close attention to his surroundings when Mellow pulled up in front of a house and parked. He wondered if it was the place that Kenny and Shay had been seen at, but then thought differently because there was no way he would just pull up on them like that. Dre was confused but didn't want to say anything. He had never been on a stakeout before, but he was almost certain that was not the way it went.

"Come on in, Dre. This will only take a minute."

"Hold up, we just gone walk in and shit gonna be cool like that? The hell is up, nigga?"

"Nah, Dre, this here is my shit. A nigga done came up since you been gone. I brought you here so we could talk a little business. You cool with that?"

"Business? You mean to tell me that you pulled me from some pussy for this? Wasn't you supposed to be taking me to where Kenny and Shay at? What happened with that?"

"Look, we gone get to that. I got a lot to tell you. Just come inside and listen to what I have to say."

Dre hesitated at first, but ultimately followed Mellow to the front door. No sooner than Mellow was about to unlock it, the door opened, and a short, thick, yellow bone honey appeared. As soon as she saw Mellow, she tiptoed and wrapped her arms around his neck. Dre tried not to look but even a blind man wouldn't be able to turn away from the beauty. Lil momma was the ultimate catch. From the top of her freshly pressed hair to the top of her manicured toes, she was perfection. The way her fat ass ate the boy shorts she had on had Dre on swole. When she noticed, she smiled deviously, but Dre turned away and covered his manhood with his hands. He couldn't let her feel like anything could go down between them because Mellow had become like family to his father and Dre would never violate that.

When the female finally loosened her hold on Mellow, she took one final glance at Dre and winked. Mellow noticed the gesture and shrugged his shoulders.

"Don't worry, Dre. She a big ass flirt, but at the end of the day, she knows that pussy belongs to me."

Dre just nodded his head and followed Mellow the rest of the way inside. He was impressed with the whole layout of the house. Mellow's crib was laced the fuck up, but what really set it off was the black baby grand piano trimmed in gold. It was an odd piece for a drug dealer to own, but Mellow had always been one to set himself apart from others, and when he noticed Dre looking at it, he went and sat down in front of it.

"This right here is my favorite piece of furniture. I used to play in church every Sunday and so having it just takes me back. A nigga needs a little something to get away from it all, and this is it for me."

Mellow put his fingers to the piano keys and began to play his rendition of "Smile" by Kirk Franklin. Dre had never been to church, but that song was familiar to everyone and could not be mistaken for anything else. He thought that Mellow actually sounded pretty good and wondered why he had never known of his talent. He never would have guessed that Mellow grew up a church boy and was puzzled at how his life took a turn and put him in the streets. Dre had always known that Mellow was different than the rest of Dory's crew and now he knew why.

"Damn, Mellow, that shit sounds good, but I ain't know you had all that in you."

"Yeah, Dre. Nobody knows, but I ain't always been a street thug. I don't tell them anything different either. I don't want them to mistake me for no weak ass punk and try my gangster. Just make sure you keep this between us, though."

"Yeah, yeah. It's all good, but ain't you tired of being somebody you're not?"

"Look, I may not be who I was meant to be, but I'm who I need to be right now. So, with that said, let's talk some business."

Mellow got up from the piano because he felt himself getting emotional. For some reason, when he thought about his growing up days, it made him that way. He trusted that Dre would keep it to himself because Dre had always been thorough. Mellow went to another door and opened it with a code from his cell phone. He looked at Dre and nodded for him to follow. The two of them walked down a set of stairs and into what looked like a man cave. The walls were covered in Cleveland Brown logos and there were no windows. There was a pool table and a mini bar and three flat screens. There were also three small sofas with a glass table in the middle. Dre had never really been into sports, but if he had that was the kind of place he would like to cheer for his favorite team in.

Mellow held out a hand and gestured for Dre to sit down. Once he was seated, Mellow pushed another code in to his phone and a small section of the wall slid open. Behind it was a large safe that Mellow walked over to and opened. Dre's eyes widened at the sight of guns and bricks of cocaine. Stacked beside the drugs was bundles of cash. The last time Dre had seen that much money was when he and Shay robbed Dory's safe. He watched as Mellow pulled out a brick and two stacks. Dre felt like he already knew what the business was about he wanted to see what Mellow had to say.

Mellow walked to the couch closest to where Dre sat and placed what he held in his hands on the table in front of him and then sat down. He hadn't told Daymion that he was contacting Tasha when he used his phone earlier that night. Mellow needed some time with Dre by himself and he felt like that was the only way to get it. He knew that Dre had been expecting his father to be with him, but so far, Dre hadn't asked why he wasn't, and Mellow hoped that it stayed that way.

"I fucked up, Dre, and your pops is going to be very disappointed about it. I told him to let's move in slow, and yet I ran in on that nigga earlier and spooked him real good. So good that he's now ghost. I went back after I left Daymion's and the house was empty. It took me a while to get that location and now I don't know what else to do, but this." Mellow points at what he had placed on the table and waited for Dre to speak.

"That ain't my life no more, Mellow. You saw that it didn't work for me the last time so you can't possibly believe that I'ma take my ass back out there again. You already know that when you do shit the same way again, you only get the same results."

"I understand that this ain't what you want to do, but I feel like it's what's going to work. Once that nigga Malachi realizes you out there, he's coming out for his revenge and that's when we are going to get him."

Dre thought about it for a minute and realized that Mellow was stating facts. Malachi was looking for a pay back and as soon as he hears that Dre was back, he would come out of hiding and seek him out. The only thing Dre was worried about was Mellow not seeing him in time. Dre wasn't afraid of dying, but he wasn't ready to be carried through cemetery gates just yet. He hoped to get a little more out of life first.

"So, what if you don't get him in time and my black ass gets smoked?"

"Dre, you have nothing to worry about. When I tell you I got your back, know that I mean it."

Dre put his hands in the praying position and rested his chin on top of them. He looked down at the drugs and money that had been placed before him. He couldn't lie to himself, he needed it, thanks to his stash being gone. True enough, he knew his father would give him all that he asked for, but Dre was a man now and wanted to make his own way. What type of respect could he gain from taking handouts? Once he settled shit with Shay, he planned on making it official with Tasha, and wondered how she would feel about him being on the block again. Just as he was about to speak, the yellow bone walked into the room and whispered something in Mellow's ear. He patted her on the ass and nodded his head and then she left the room. Dre wondered what it was about but decided to mind his own business. He figured that if Mellow wanted him to know, he would tell him on his own.

"What about a weapon? I can't go out there without a strap."

"Say no more, I got you."

Mellow stood and went back to his safe and pulled out a nine-millimeter along with an ammo-filled clip. He reached in a little further and pulled out a fresh box of backup ammo just in case. He wanted to make sure Dre was good all the way around. He walked back over to Dre and turned the handle of the gun to him. Dre reached out and gripped it like it was meant just for him.

"This is perfect. My favorite piece."

"Anything else you need, just let me know, but you have to make me one promise. Don't say anything to your father about what we got going on."

"Why is it a secret? I thought you two were straight."

"We are, but he don't want you in the game. It took a lot just to convince him that we needed you to get to Malachi."

"It's not going to take pops long to find out that I'm out there slanging. What am I supposed to tell him when he questions it?"

"You a man now, Dre. you'll figure it out. Now, come on so I can take you back to Tasha. I got other shit I need to do."

Dre stood along with Mellow and the two of them nodded at each other, acknowledging their understanding. Mellow walked back to the safe and pulled out a small duffel bag and threw it across the room to Dre. he caught it with one hand and then bent over to pick his new reality up to put it in the bag. Mellow shut the safe and then punched the code in his cell to close the wall, and then the two of them went back upstairs. Dre didn't see the yellow bone but he somehow felt like she already knew what was up. He bet she was the type of chic that kept her mouth shut because he doubted that Mellow would have fucked with her if she didn't. Mellow was the type of nigga that would rather be single than fuck with a disloyal, big mouth bitch and he was the same way when it came to choosing friends. Dre trusted Mellow and that was the only reason he agreed to go along with his plan.

Mellow drove the speed limit through the city streets to take Dre back to the hotel. He couldn't afford to get pulled over for some bullshit, so he was being cautious. The streetlights shined just enough for him to see the worry on Dre's face. He knew that Dre had been through so much in his short life, but Mellow felt like he had the strength to carry on. Every obstacle Dre faced had brought him to where he was now, and as long as Mellow had air in his lungs, he would protect him along with Daymion.

"Why you so quiet over there? You must have something to say."

Dre turned his head and looked at Mellow. He had so much shit running through his mental and now the thought of going back out to the block added to it. He had a good mind to tell Mellow that he changed his mind, but he didn't want to miss any opportunity to get Malachi. The nigga was going to have to see him one way or the other.

"Just wondering how Tasha is going to feel about me being in the streets again. I mean, a nigga gotta do something to keep food on the table. Right?"

"I can assure you that even without those streets, Tasha, or your father ain't gone let you go hungry. Shit, you know Tasha do her own thing in the game. She's one of Daymion's top people. You set, baby boy, either way you turn."

"What you mean, she's one of his top people? The fuck is you talking about?"

Mellow knew he had fucked up. He thought that Tasha would have told him that she worked for his father, but it was obvious that she didn't. "You mean Tasha didn't tell you that she pushes for Daymion?"

"Hell nah, she ain't told me no shit like that. No wonder she riding in luxury cars and sliding black cards through credit card machines. That should have been the first thing out of her mouth when she picked me up, but it's all good. I'ma get some answers, not only from her, but from him too. That shit ain't cool."

"Come on, Dre, ain't nothing to be upset about. Daymion has held Tasha down the entire time you been gone. He even tried to talk her out of doing it, but she was determined. When he finally let her in, he realized that she was pretty damn good at it and the rest is history. You got a loyal ass female on your team, Dre. Don't fuck that up."

Dre didn't respond to what Mellow had said, but he knew once again that he was right. Tasha had needed someone while he was away and turning to his father may have been the best thing for her. She had switched out on her own brother for Dre and there were certain things she couldn't turn to her grandmother for. Dre was confused though. He didn't understand why she didn't tell him everything herself. He shouldn't have had to hear it from the next man. Dre wondered what else she hadn't told him and couldn't wait to ask her.

When Mellow pulled back up at the hotel, Tasha's car was gone. Dre knew that she had been feeling some type of way about him leaving, but she didn't have to do him dirty like that. He didn't want to have to stay at his father's house, but he had no other choice because he had left the room key with Tasha. Mellow noticed the look on Dre's face and decided to rescue him from his issue.

"You know, I could take you to her house if you want. It's not that far away."

"Her house? The fuck? Anything else you wanna enlighten me on? Because it seems like she don't want me to know shit."

"Chill, Dre. Maybe she was just waiting for the right time."

"The right time? Nigga, don't you think the right time would have been as soon as she picked me up? Bruh, I ain't got time for that shit."

Mellow just shook his head and continued to dive the short distance to Tasha's house. He knew that Dre didn't want to hear shit else he had to say anyway. Hell, he had already said too much. Mellow had never been the type of nigga to tell peoples business, but he thought Tasha would have already told him. She wasn't going to be happy about it, but it was too late to take it back. When he pulled up in front of her house, he looked over at Dre and gave him one more word of advice.

"Aye, yo, take it easy on her. They don't make them like her anymore."

Dre let out a small chuckle and got out. He waited for Mellow to drive away before he approached the front door. He wondered why Tasha let him take her to a hotel when she had her own crib. He didn't need a woman in his life that was going to keep secrets. That shit was flaw as fuck to him. He stood at her front door and was about to ring the bell when suddenly it opened, and Tasha stood in front of him with her hands on her hips and an attitude on her face.

"I should have known that Mellow would bring you here. You might as well come in."

"Well, what I'm trying to figure out is why he was the one who told me, and I don't want to hear that shit about waiting for the right time. You didn't think that the first thing I should have known was that you were pushing drugs for my father? When the hell was gonna be the right time, Tasha?"

"You're right, Dre, I'm sorry. I should have told you. I had plenty of opportunity. I just didn't know how."

"Fuck you mean? You should have just spit that shit out and got it over with. Do you know how it makes me feel for another nigga to tell me what's going on with my bitch?"

"Oh, so you call yourself claiming me now? You trying to say this shit between us is official?"

Tasha stood in front of him with her hands on her hips and smiled at Dre. He wanted to stay mad at her, but he just didn't have it in him. He looked her up and down and then put his hand on his dick. Her attitude had him like stone and there was no way he could curb it. His sexual desire for her couldn't be tamed. Tasha had grown up to be all woman and all he wanted to do was gas up and drive along all her curves. He knew that he was going to have his hands full when it came to her, but Tasha was that bitch, and she knew it.

"You know what? Fuck it."

With that said, Dre pulled Tasha close to him. She tried to play hard and resist him but, in her mind, she had always belonged to him and there would be no way she could deny him. She wanted to make sure he would never run to Shay. She grabbed his hand and led him to her massive bedroom, and slowly stripped off what little she had on and then she helped him take off his own clothes. When they got in the bed, things started off a little slow, due to each of their inexperience, but once they found their rhythm, it was like fireworks went off. Dre never knew that he could feel so good, but Tasha put it on him. She realized that he really was worth the wait, and she would wait all over again if she had to. When they were done, they spent the rest of the night in each other's arms. They wanted to enjoy every minute they could because with Malachi Jensen still out there, they never knew when it would be their last.

Chapter 9

Malachi drove slowly through his old stomping grounds. The plain looking Ford Explorer he pushed was something he never would have been caught dead in, but it was not the time to be flashy. That day would come soon enough. He still had the conversation with Shay on his mind. He couldn't believe she had the nerve to think that him and Daymion could ever be cool. Too much damage had been done and no amount of truce could fix it. However, Malachi had no choice but to get back out on the block. He couldn't do it like he used to though, because he had to start from scratch.

Malachi thought back to when he first hit the streets. He was a young thug on the rise and although it took him a while to make a name for himself, he eventually earned his spot, but along with his spot, there would come haters, and therefore, he had to be on his toes at all times. Once he met Malia, shit started turning even more sour. She had been every dope man's dream but he somehow managed to pull her. Malachi felt like he was on top of the world and then, his life began to fall apart. Malia no longer belonged to just him and the day she got killed, it brought out something that had been in him all along. Malachi became a terror to everyone around him. People used to fear him, but in the end, he became the one in fear.

He would never admit it to anyone, but Malachi didn't want to face off against Daymion Myers. He was well aware of how Daymion got down and how far his reach was,

Malachi was shocked that the nigga hadn't found him yet, but he was no fool he knew that Daymion would never give up. Going into hiding made Malachi feel like a pussy, but he'd had no other options at the time. Daymion was a mufucka you had to hide from if you wanted to keep on breathing.

Malachi played tough around Shay because he wanted her to respect him and not look at him as weak. He had tried for years to top Daymion's status, but Malachi just couldn't make the cut. It was only when Daymion got locked up that the door opened up for him. Once Daymion hit the streets again, Malachi knew it would only be a matter of time before he took back over. Killing Kiara was not part of his plan but with Daymion free, he would soon lose her too. However, the person he really wanted to get a hold of was Dre. That little nigga had nerve to put a death wish over Malachi's head. Had it not been for his partner being in the bed with Kiara, Dre would have already got to him.

Malachi had grown tired of driving around, so he pulled over to the side of the road and lit a blunt. He had planned to only take a couple of pulls. Just enough to clear his mind so he could think straight. The weed had him feeling relaxed and before he realized it, he had smoked the whole thing.

Malachi looked out the window and saw a young, fine honey about to walk past him. He had never seen her before so that meant she didn't know who he was. It had been a while since he had been up in some pussy and so he figured he would try his luck. He rolled his window down as soon as she was beside it.

"Aye, lil momma. You feel like chillin' with a nigga for a little while?"

The female stopped in her tracks and looked at Malachi like he was crazy. She had never seen him before, so she took a second and looked him in the eyes. She stepped a little closer to his vehicle and when she smelled the freshly smoked Kush, her stomach did flips. She wondered if he had anything else to go with it, because even though she liked weed. She needed something a little more potent.

"Depends on what you mean by chillin'."

"The fuck is that supposed to mean? Come on, I got some good ass weed that will put you on your toes, and some even better dick that will put you on your back. What do you say?"

"Mmm. Well, the weed sounds all good, but I need something else to set me off. You ain't holding no *hard*?"

"Yeah, get on in. I got just what you need."

The female smiled and rushed around to the passenger side and got in. Malachi was a little disappointed because from the looks of her, he never would have dubbed her a crackhead. That was just his luck, though, and he figured that he might as well make the best of the situation. He locked the doors just to be safe and unzipped his pants. When he pulled his dick out, the female smacked her lips and rolled her eyes. He usually couldn't stand that ghetto shit, but he needed a nut and was willing to compromise. He stroked his dick a few times and then reached over to try and cop a feel, but the female pushed his hand away.

"Uh-uh. You got to give me my shit up front. I'ont know you like that."

"Aiight. I got you but don't smoke this shit in my ride. I can't stand the smell and I ain't trying to inhale none."

"Well, if I don't try it out, how I'm supposed to know that it's even real?"

"You just gone have to trust me or get out and carry on to wherever it was you was going."

The thought of losing out on a hit made her rethink her options. She had been walking around for over an hour looking for a trick and had almost given up until Malachi stopped her. He seemed real enough, so she decided to handle her business and smoke her shit when she was done.

"Alright. You seem like a good guy, so I'ma trust you. I ain't giving up the pussy though, but I'll suck your dick real good."

Malachi decided to settle for what he could get because he was growing frustrated with the female. He nodded his head in agreement and leaned back a little. When he felt her warm mouth on his manhood, he closed his eyes and moaned in pleasure. He had to give it to the bitch, she could suck a mean dick. She had him ready to nut in only four minutes. He was impressed because it usually took him longer. When he came in her mouth, he expected her to stop and spit it out, but the bitch was a thoroughbred. She swallowed each and every drop, and even licked him clean. Malachi opened his eyes and sat his seat up. He knew that with the head being that good, the pussy had to be even better. He was about to try and talk her into spending the night with him at a motel but before he could ask, he saw something he hadn't been expecting.

It had been a few years, and the nigga had matured in looks, but there was no mistake. He could have recognized him from anywhere. Malachi wondered just how long the mufucka had been out. He was a little shocked that Dre was alone because he had to have known that he had a contract over his head. Daymion was a fool for putting the bastard back out there but he would soon learn from that mistake. Malachi was stuck on the fact that he was that close to the nigga who had been aiming for his head. It was a violation that couldn't go unpunished. He was so entranced with Dre, that he forgot about the female he had beside him.

"Hello. Hey, you staring at that nigga mighty hard. I hope you ain't into dick too. I think that is so disgusting."

Malachi turned his head to look at her and became hard all over again. She was a pretty ass crackhead, and he wondered if he could clean her up and make her his bitch, but then he thought about the drama it would bring to his life. He hadn't met one woman yet who could keep her mouth shut and her panties up, so he decided to just stick with his plan and keep her for the night. He knew that if Dre was out there once, he'd be back out there again, and Malachi needed to plan his strategy.

"You know, you got a foul ass mouth, but I like it, and I ain't ready to let you go just yet, so what you say? You wanna chill with a nigga for the rest of the night?"

"Hell nah. You already ain't letting me smoke. Shit, I'm trying to feel like I'm floating on cloud nine, but you got me up in this ride at a standstill."

"I'll tell you what. How 'bout I get us a room and put a few more stones in your hand. You gone be okay with that?"

"Well, I guess so. I am tired of being out here and wouldn't mind kicking back, but that dick better be all you said it was or I'm out."

"Oh, it's gonna be all that and more. A nigga like me don't give disappointment."

With that said, Malachi took one final look at Dre and started his ride. He was ready to fuck something up, and that night, he would have to settle for some pussy. He pushed his whip to the cheapest motel he could find. He thought the female would have something slick to say about it, but he figured it had been the only type of place that she had been used to. He knew how niggas were, hell he was one of them, and he wasn't about to pay her in drugs and drop a whole lot of gwop on an expensive room, even if it was for the night.

Malachi pulled out forty bucks and handed it to her so she could go pay for a room. He couldn't afford to take the chance of someone he had known from before seeing him, especially in such a trashy place. Hell, he might have been close to broke, but no one else needs to know that. When the female took the money from his hand, she put it down her bra as if she were going to keep it, but Malachi let her know immediately that she better not try him.

"You putting that in there like it's yours, and even though you don't know me, I hope you at least know better. I am not the one to fuck over."

"You don't have to worry, I ain't the robbing type. I'll bring you back the change. Oh, and by the way, my name is Diane."

"Thanks, but I didn't ask."

She smacked her lips and got out without another word. Malachi couldn't understand what the problem was. He only brought her to the motel to fuck, not become friends, so anything personal about her was irrelevant to him. He decided to light another blunt while he waited on her. He knew that he should be easy on his stash until he came up, but one more wouldn't hurt him. No sooner than he lit it, he saw Diane walking back to the ride. She didn't even bother to get back in, but instead, went to the driver's side and held a room key up in one hand, and Malachi's change in the other. He thought maybe she wasn't that bad after all.

Malachi took a long pull of the blunt and then sat it in the ashtray. He was going in that room to fuck, not get high, and so the only thing he needed was a condom. He reached over to the glove box and pulled out a package of magnums. He couldn't take the risk of catching something and didn't know how many other niggas he was about to fuck behind. When he stopped breathing, it would be a bullet that would take him out, not some sick pussy.

He walked behind Diane as she sashayed to the room. He couldn't wait to get in that ass and only hoped it was worth his time. Once she opened the door, a foul stench hit Malachi in the nose. He wondered how often the room had been cleaned, or if it had ever been cleaned at all. It definitely was a trap spot and since that was what he was there for, he figured he would make the best of it.

As soon as Diane shut the door and locked it. Malachi reached in his pocket and pulled out his crack. He took a couple of more stones and handed it to her. He noticed that he didn't have that many left, so what he gave her would have to suffice. When he handed them to her, she seemed okay with it, so he put the rest back in his jeans.

"Yo, I hope this is good for you, 'cause I ain't got much left on me."

"This is actually more than anyone else would have given me, but do you mind if I take a hit now?"

"Nah, go 'head and do your thing. Maybe it will take away the odor in here. But do me a favor and get undressed first. A nigga wanna play in that pussy while you get your high on."

Diane did just what Malachi asked and then sat up on the bed against the headboard with her legs spread. Malachi looked at her fat pussy and smiled. His dick immediately hardened at the sight. He waited until she put the flame from the lighter to the stem and then slid a finger inside of her. She was wet and slippery, just the way he liked it. He slid in and out of her a couple of times and then pulled his finger out. When he put his finger under his nose to smell it, he jerked his head back. Her pussy smelled like a fishpond. Malachi scrunched up his nose and stood. He was pissed. He couldn't believe that she had the audacity to be out tricking with a dirty pussy. She could have at least cleaned up after her last trick.

"Damn. When was the last time you put soap and water in that hole? Shit smells a little fishy down there. Your ass got to do something about that."

"I was on my way to wash up until you stopped me."

He could tell that she was a little embarrassed, but he didn't give a damn. She should have taken better care of herself. He always thought that the tricks walked around with some kind of wipes to clean themselves up, but he realized that he had been wrong.

"Oh, so you gone blame that foul ass pussy on me? Look, that shit done fucked up my mood but I'ma let you have that. Next time I see you, though, it's on you so don't try to make up some lame ass excuse of why you can't pay up."

Diane gave him no response because honestly, she was just too high to do so. Malachi gave her one last glance and walked out of the room. He usually would have beat a bitch ass about his shit, but he didn't want to bring himself any unnecessary drama. He had other things that he needed to handle. Ones that didn't involve a bitch.

When Malachi got back in his ride, he started the engine and then pulled the rest of his blunt from the ashtray. He took a long pull and held the smoke in until he pulled out of the parking lot. He only took a couple of more pulls before putting it back out. He felt like he'd had enough for one night. The effects of the weed had him hungry as hell, but instead of driving somewhere to get a bite to eat, Malachi drove back to the block. He just wanted to take one more look at the mufucka, but when he got there, he was disappointed to see that Dre had left. He drove around for a little while, checking other spots, just to be sure he didn't overlook him, but he came up empty handed. He decided to take it in for the night, but he would be back and when he returned, he would make sure he was ready, because paying Dre back for attempting to kill him was an opportunity he refused to miss.

Chapter 10

Kayla met Dre at the front door and pulled him in for a hug. He was not her son, but he was as close to one as she would ever get. She and Daymion had tried for over a year to have a child of their own but kept coming up short. They had become so frustrated with it that they finally went to a specialist to find out what the problem was. It turned out that Kayla couldn't reproduce. She and Daymion had talked about seeking other options, but decided in the end that they were fine with just the two of them. They didn't need a child to define their love for one another. Instead, they hoped that one day, Dre would settle down and give them some grandchildren. They just hadn't shared the idea with him yet.

Kayla could tell that Dre was annoyed by being called over. He had been out on the block doing his thing when he got the call on the new cell phone Tasha had given him. Dre wasn't crazy about the phone, he actually felt like he could live without it. He felt like having the phone was just another avenue for people to bother him and there was nothing he hated worse than being aggravated. He could tell from the look on Kayla's face that Daymion was about to hit his last nerve.

"Please don't tell me I'm here on some bullshit, because I don't have time for that."

"I'm not gonna tell you anything, Dre. That's not my place. Just hear your father out."

With that said, Kayla turned and walked away. He knew Kayla didn't want to get in the middle of whatever him and Daymion had going on and he understood why. She loved both of them and didn't want to be put in a position to take sides. That would be unfair to her. After Kayla walked away, Dre almost turned around to walk back out of the house, but he felt like it would make him look like a pussy. He wasn't about to spend his time avoiding Daymion and he needed him to realize that he couldn't run his life.

Dre walked slowly to Daymion's office not because he was afraid, but because he wanted to take his time and look around. He hadn't taken much notice when he had been there before, but he saw that his father was living large. He had invested his money well, but Dre thought that all that space was a waste. He had always wondered why big dealers had to advertise what they had. That was how mufuckas got robbed. Dre had never cared about rising in the dope game. Hell, he was just fine where he was at. He had only stepped back out in hopes of bringing Malachi out and once he accomplished that goal, he would wash his hands of it all.

Daymion was sitting cross legged in his leather swivel chair with his Giorgio Armani house slippers on when Dre walked in. The expensive house coat and pajamas seemed to match his demeanor. Dre couldn't deny it. His father was fly, but he wasn't impressed, he just wanted to get things over with, because for some reason, he didn't feel very welcome.

"It's late, and from the looks of your wardrobe, you should be in bed, so why am I here?"

Daymion uncrossed his legs and leaned forward. He placed his elbows on his knees and looked up at Dre with a look that could kill. Dre felt chills up his spine, but he wasn't scared. It had been a long time since he had been scared of a mufucka. He could hold his own. Even against his father.

"You want to explain to me why you out on the corner selling that shit? Come on, Dre, you haven't even been home a week and you already puttin' yourself out like that. The hell is wrong with you?"

"First off, I ain't gotta explain shit to you. In case you have forgotten, I'm grown. If you wanted to run something and raise me right, then you should have thought of that beforehand. You don't get to dictate a damn thing in my life so remember your place the next time you dial my number."

Daymion stood and walked up on Dre until they were face to face. There was no way that he could let the disrespect go. If he did, it would continue on. Dre was his son, not some nigga in the streets and Daymion was tired of him acting like one.

"My place? I'm still your father, Dre, whether I was there for you or not, and you will not stand here and disrespect me. You do not have to be out there in them streets like you were before. I agreed to let you in on the plan to pull Malachi out, but I did not agree for you to be out there slangin' dope."

"No, you didn't, but I did and I'm gonna keep going out there until I don't want to go anymore. Now if you want to be a father, be a fucking father. I don't need a boss."

Daymion backed away from him as soon as Dre said those words. He understood the message behind what he said. Daymion had waited so long to be in Dre's life and now that he was, he had been so busy making demands that he didn't realize Dre needed him in ways that a son needs a father. Instead of spending time getting to know his seed and building a relationship with him Daymion had been playing boss and treating Dre like a nigga that worked for him. He hadn't realized it until Dre pointed it out, but he was going to change it now that he knew.

"Ya know what, Dre? You right. I haven't been much of a father to you. Not then, and honestly, not even now. I have an excuse for not being there when you was growing up but I don't have one for now. I apologize for that, but you ain't been around since you been out. I don't know why you staying away, but you ain't got to worry. I won't abandon you again."

Dre stared at Daymion without speaking. He was his father's mirror but he was nothing like him. Daymion was a man that demanded respect just from his presence alone and Dre felt so far beneath him. Kiara had raised him to despise the man who planted him but how could he hate someone he admired so much. The more she kept him from Daymion, the more Dre wanted him in his life. True enough, Dre had avoided his father as much as he could in the short time that he had been free. He was afraid that Daymion wouldn't like the way he had turned out, but instead of trying to fix things in his own brokenness, he was more concerned with taking Malachi Jensen's life. He would do whatever it took, even if it cost him his last heartbeat.

"We good pops, and eventually, we gone get to where we need to be, but right now, you gotta let me find my own way.

"I understand all that, but I still don't want you out in them streets. I can provide you with everything you need. You and Tasha."

"Yeah? Well from what I understand, you been providing for Tasha. Got her pushing shit like she a nigga, but as of today, she's through."

"So, it's like that? You come home and regulate the life of a bitch you don't even want? You don't give a damn about Tasha. You too hooked on that bastard's daughter, even after she betrayed you and me. Is that what you out there for? Huh? You want her to hear that you out so she can come running to you? You think she's gonna come alone? As long as you out there, you're a fucking target."

"Nah. As long as I carry your name, it makes me a target. Whether I'm in the streets or not. Shay wouldn't do me dirty like that. I know her better than anyone, and until I see her and handle our unfinished business, I won't rest."

"And what about Tasha? You just gone put her on the sidelines again?"

"Tasha's good, so don't worry about her. Besides, I don't hear her complaining. She knows her place in my life, but she also knows that I can't just push Shay out of my head, and I know that if I wouldn't have gotten locked up, she never would have pulled that dumb shit with Malachi. She never would have betrayed me like that. I know she had her reasons for doing what she did , but I need to find out exactly what those reasons were. I need closure pops and I ain't moving on until I get it."

"So, in the meantime, you string Tasha along. You and I both know how that girl feels about you, but it's obvious you ain't feeling the same way. You ain't doing nothing but giving her false hope and you wrong. You have no right to run shit going on in her life. She enjoys what she is doing and not only that, she's damn good at it."

"Dealing in drugs and being a fucking mule is not the life for her."

"Then give her a better one. Give her what she deserves. That girl has lived and breathed for you for years and if you can't see what you got beside you, something is wrong."

Dre thought about what Daymion had said. He knew that Tasha's feelings were real, but as bad as he wanted to entertain them, he couldn't. At least, not completely. Not when he still had Shay digging in his mental. He couldn't let go of his desire for her and wondered how she had managed to get such a strong hold on him. Dre was about to answer his father, but Kayla's voice stopped him.

"Daymion, honey, why don't you call it a night and come to bed? It's late and I'm sure that Dre is tired and he's more than welcome to stay."

"Thanks, but I got Tasha waiting on me and I've already been gone too long as it is, so I'ma have to pass. Maybe next time, though."

Dre looked at his father and nodded and then turned away. He walked up to Kayla and gave her a kiss on the cheek. She had always managed to save him right on time. Dre told himself that the next time Daymion's number shows on his screen, he's sending it to voicemail. He wasn't going to waste his time listening to anymore demands, not only from Daymion, but from anyone.

Once Kayla heard the front door close, she walked over to Daymion and gave him a hug he looked like he needed. She didn't want to dip in his business, but she knew his mind was heavy and all she wanted to do was lighten his load. "You wanna tell me about it? Maybe I can help."

"I know you don't mind, but I really don't want to burden you with my bullshit."

"That's what I'm here for, Daymion. So go ahead and get it off your chest."

"Dre's back out on the block and that's the one place he knows I don't want him. It's like he's doing shit to defy me. I don't know what else to think."

"Maybe you need to stop with the things you want and ask him what it is he wants, and whether you agree with his choices or not, you stand by him. Dre's used to being on his own and not having someone to care about him. Now that he does have someone, he doesn't know what to do with it. Just go slow, Daymion, and show him that you are not going to abandon him again. He will come around. I'm sure of it."

Even though Daymion listened to Kayla's advice, it didn't mean he was going to follow it. Dre was his only seed, and he only wanted to protect him, especially from the streets and the dangers that lurk in the darkness. He wondered if Mellow might have had a hand in pushing Dre back out there. He remembered that Mellow had used his phone to make a call. Was it Tasha or Dre he had called? Daymion was going to be pissed if he found it to be true. He didn't want to believe that his partner would go behind his back like that, but he knew that Mellow and Dre had history from when they both worked for Dory. he would make damn sure to give Mellow a call and find out if he had a part to play in the whole thing.

When Daymion and Mellow had been locked up together, they spent many days and nights talking. Mellow was well aware of how he felt about Dre being on the block, so for Mellow to betray him would be the ultimate let down.

Daymion had so much shit going on his thoughts that it made it hard for him to fall asleep that night. He held Kayla close beside him as he looked to the ceiling. He couldn't imagine a life without her or Dre, but he was being put in a position he didn't want to be in. Dre wouldn't listen to him and because of that, everything Daymion loved was in danger. He didn't want to have to pull out the big guns and hit the corners again, but that may have been just what he had to do. Somebody had to fall, he just hoped it wasn't him.

Chapter 11

Dre stood under the short eave of the roof on the side of the building he had been serving in front of. He was trying to protect himself from the thunderous rain that had been coming down for over twenty minutes. Had he known the weather was going to be like that, he would have stayed in for the night. He thought of a lot of other things he would rather be doing at a time like that. Things that would give him much more pleasure than what he was getting that night. Dre was certain that the brand new Jordans he had on his feet would be ruined by the downpour, and as much as he hated to see money go to waste, there wasn't shit he could do about it.

The block was on fire and the fiends had been coming back-to-back. Some of them remembered him from before, which was what he had hoped for. He needed word to get out in order for him and Mello's plans to work. The storm seemed to have slowed the fiends down a bit, but Dre knew that as soon as it let up, they would be back in full force. He had plenty of drugs in his possession and would be waiting for their return.

Being back out on the grind had been no fun at all for him and the only thing that kept him out there was the possibility of making the enemy show his face. So far, shit had been quiet, and Dre was growing more and more impatient with each day that passed. Mellow had sworn to him that the plan would work, but Dre wasn't so sure about that. Tasha had tried to talk him into letting her go out with him, but he told her that a woman's place wasn't in the streets. He knew that she only wanted to follow behind him out of fear of him running into Shay. She wouldn't admit it herself, but Dre knew he was right.

Thoughts of his intense meeting with Daymion crossed his mind. He knew that his father was only trying to protect him, but Dre didn't need his protection. He just needed to be left alone so he could handle what Daymion should have handled long ago. If he wanted to be there, he should have thought about that while Dre was growing up, because now, it was too late. Dre never even really knew how to be a man until he got locked up himself, so Daymion's attempts at being a father were a little late.

Once Dre realized that the rain had lightened up, he stepped back out on post. He looked around but didn't notice anyone else and wondered if all the other niggas had called it a night. Dre shrugged his shoulders and leaned back against the wall. He figured he would give it one more hour and then go in. He told Tasha that he would be in early, but he knew it was a lie as soon as he said it. The streets made Dre feel free even though it was the one place that could cause him to lose his freedom all over again.

Dre pulled a pack of Newports from his back pocket and put one in his mouth. He couldn't recall when smoking had become a habit, but somehow, it had. No one else knew he did it, and he wanted to keep it that way. Tasha told him one night that he smelled like an ashtray but he put it off on the niggas hanging around the block. Dre hated the smell of the cigarettes, but he enjoyed the smoothness of the menthol flavor on his taste buds. He lit the one he had in between his lips and leaned back against the wall, but before he was halfway through his smoke break, he heard a familiar voice.

"Hey? Hey, you holding? I got twenty to spend."

Dre couldn't believe his eyes when he looked up and saw Kenny in front of him. It had only been a couple of weeks since he ran into him behind the house where he had looked for his money sash, but Kenny looked like a completely different version of himself. Dre shook his head at the sight of him and waited to see if he recognized him too, but realized that Kenny was so drugged out that he didn't know who he was talking to. Dre's nose flared and as bad as he wanted to beat his ass, he couldn't. He wanted to wait until the mufucka was sober because he wanted Kenny to feel every punch and kick he gave him.

"Yeah. I got a little something, but you sure a twenty is all you want?"

"That's all I can stand right now, but if you give me a nice piece, as soon as I hit a lick, I'll make sure to come back and spend my money with you."

"A lick, huh? What kind of lick you 'bout to come up on?"

"Now, you know I can't tell you all that, but I can assure you, it's gonna be a damn good one."

"Aiight, but don't let me find out you come up and then go spend your money with the next nigga."

"Come on now. I give you my word."

Dre pulled the package out of his pocket and picked out the biggest rock he had. He passed it over to Kenny in exchange for the crumpled up twenty-dollar bill. He watched as Kenny examined the piece of dope, and from the way he licked his dry, crusty lips, Dre knew he was satisfied with what he had been given. Kenny smiled and closed his hand into a fist to make sure he didn't drop his piece of dope, and then he walked off without saying another word. Dre had a good mind to follow him but didn't think it would be a smart move. He knew the time would come when they would meet up again, so he decided to wait a little longer.

Not long after Kenny left, Dre felt himself getting drowsy and figured that he should take it in. He had done pretty good that night so there was no sense in being greedy. He took one last pull off his Newport and then flicked it on the ground. He hoped that by the time he made it home to Tasha the putrid smell of the cigarette smoke would be gone. He didn't feel like hearing her bitch about the stench.

As soon as Dre took a step to leave, a pearl white Lexus with dark tinted windows pulled up beside him. He had never seen the ride before and when the passenger side window started to go down, his paranoia kicked in. He thought it was a hit until the voice that came from inside caused him to freeze up.

"Excuse me. I'm looking for Kenny. Have you seen him out here anywhere? I haven't heard from him in days and it's starting to worry me."

"Now see, if you would have kept it real with a nigga like me you wouldn't be out here looking for the next one."

Dre leaned down and stuck his head through the open window and as soon as he looked Shay in the eyes, his emotions took a hit. She was still as beautiful as the first day he met her, and he suddenly forgot all about getting home to Tasha. All he wanted to do was get in the car and ride away with the woman he had given his heart to. He knew it was wrong to stand there and lust after her, but he just couldn't help himself.

"Dre? Is that you?"

"Sup, Shay? It's a damn shame that you ain't even recognize me. Shows how much you gave a fuck about a nigga, but it's all good, because I was fine without you."

"Look, Dre, I'm sorry. I know that I should have been there for you, but there was no way I could have explained that to my father. He would have never understood."

"But he understands you out here looking for Kenny's cracked out ass. That shit you and him doing is flaw as fuck, Shay. How the hell you gone fuck with a nigga I rolled with? That shit ain't right."

"It was something that just happened, Dre. It wasn't no underhanded shit. I was lonely and he came along. I needed someone. I didn't know what else to do."

"Yeah? Well, that's a lame ass excuse. You sure you ain't do it as payback for trying to put a bullet in your old man's dome? I'm pissed about hitting the wrong man because Malachi deserved it for the way he done me and my momma, and if I would have known he was your pops, it wouldn't have changed a damn thing."

"I know how you feel about him, Dre, but I can't help who my father is."

"Yeah? Well, that don't mean you gotta be like him and roll on his side. The fuck is your loyalty at?"

"Look, I know you're disappointed in me, but I don't want no tension between us, so can we please go somewhere else and talk? We have some catching up to do."

Dre knew he should have turned around and walked away, but he just couldn't do it. He needed to hear what Shay had to say because he couldn't move forward until he did. He knew that it sounded foolish to profess his love for someone he had never even been intimate with, but for Shay, he didn't mind playing a fool. He just hoped that playing one didn't get him killed.

Chapter 12

Malachi sat there and tried to comprehend what he had seen. He'd been sitting in the same spot every night just so he could keep an eye on Dre. He had been so focused on him that he'd forgotten why he went back out there in the first place. His funds were steadily depleting and had Malachi thinking about pulling a jack move. He was almost certain that he could con one of the young hustlers into believing that he could turn them on to bigger things if only they would invest in the start-up. Malachi had always had one hell of a talk game but he had to put all thoughts to the side so he could focus on what was in front of him.

Malachi had been ready to take it in for the night and was about to leave until he saw Shay pull up to Dre and let her window down. He watched closely to make sure she wasn't in harm's way and that's when he realized she looked a little too comfortable talking to him. He decided it appeared that way because of the distance he was from them.

After all, it was dark out and the streetlights weren't that bright. He just couldn't imagine anyone who had his blood running through their veins being friendly with the enemy. Malachi laughed at himself for even thinking something so absurd, but then, he watched Dre get into Shay's ride.

Malachi thought back to the moment when Shay tried to convince him to call a truce with Daymion. He thought she was just trying to stop the drama so he could feel safer, but Malachi now wondered if it had been because of Dre. The mere thought of his daughter having any kind of feeling toward a Myers made him sick on his stomach. Malachi didn't know what was going on so he didn't want to move too fast. He would feel like shit if something happened to her because of him.

Malachi continued to watch, and when Shay pulled off, he pulled off behind her. He followed at a safe distance even though the vehicle was a disguise, and he knew Shay would never be able to recognize it. Malachi began to feel like he was replaying an episode he'd once had with Malia. He remembered the first time he had seen her with Dory. He had felt like someone punched him in the heart and caused it to burst. She had meant everything to him and the thoughts of another man anywhere near her made him want to kill someone. Shay was all he had left from his time with Malia, and he wanted to protect her, but if he found out she had betrayed him, he would be the one to take her last breath. He wished that he had a way of listening to what was being said between Shay and Dre at that moment, but since he didn't, he decide he would use another tactic.

Malachi picked up his phone and dialed Shay's number. He expected her to pick up immediately like she usually did, but when it continued to ring, he became angry. He knew that she was probably trying to think of a quick lie to tell him and it disappointed him. When Shay finally answered, Malachi was at his breaking point.

"What the hell took you so long to answer? You always answer my calls immediately. What's going on with that?"

"Chill out, dad. I was on the other line with Tara. Why are you tripping on me like that?"

Tara was Shay's closest friend. She had met her shortly after Malachi got her to leave town with him. He had done his homework on Tara for Shay's safety but never found anything that would be alarming, so he never put up a fuss or said anything when Shay mentioned her. However, he knew that Shay was lying to him, and he knew why.

"Tara, huh? What y'all talked about that was so important that you couldn't answer my call?"

"What's with all the questions? Did you forget that I'm grown or something? Look, I don't know what's up with you right now but I gotta go. I'm tired and on my way to the apartment to get some rest. I'll call you in the morning."

Before Malachi could say another word, Shay hung up on him; a move he found totally disrespectful and one she had never made before. He wondered if Dre had made her do it or if she had done it on her own, and hoped it wasn't the latter.

When Shay's ride pulled into a hotel parking lot, he pulled in behind her but when she stopped in front of the office, Malachi continued to drive past. He parked in a spot he could watch her from and prepared his weapon just in case he needed to use it, and then, he waited to see what would happen next.

Shay walked out of the hotel office and got back in her ride. Malachi's nose flared in anger as he watched Shay pull into a parking spot and get out, along with Dre. She seemed to be content with who she was with and it caused Malachi to wonder just how long the two of them had been cordial. All of Malachi's questions were answered when Shay opened the room door and turned to smile at Dre. A stranger would think the two of them were in love, but Malachi refused to entertain the thought. When the room door shut behind the couple, Malachi was left to his own imagination, which had never been a good thing.

The one thing he hoped would never happen, did, right in front of him he wondered how long his own daughter had been lying to him, but then decided that it didn't matter because it would be her last lie. Malachi started his vehicle and drove away from the hotel. He couldn't stand to sit there any longer and not do nothing. There was a time and place for everything and when that time came, Malachi would be ready, whether anyone else was or not.

Chapter 13

Kayla crossed her arms over her chest and watched as Daymion paced. She hated to see him that way, but she understood what he was going through. He'd had big expectations of how things would be when Dre got home and yet, nothing had turned out the way he had planned it. The street life had never been what he wanted for Dre, although Daymion still lived it himself. True enough, he wanted Dre to one day run his empire, but it was a position that would keep him behind the scenes, and out of harm's way. His only problem was that he'd never asked Dre what he wanted.

The ringing of the doorbell stopped Daymion in his tracks. He already knew who was at the door, because he'd asked them to come over. He needed a sit down so he could get some answers, and even if he had to force them, he would get what he wanted.

Mellow walked in with his hands in his pockets but Daymion wasn't intimidated by the stance. No matter what the two of them had been through, their beef would never come to gunplay. Him and Mellow had a mutual respect for one another, even though at that moment Daymion felt like he had been stabbed in the back.

"You want to explain to me what happened with the stake out and why you have my son back in the streets? You knew that was the one place I never wanted him at, so why the hell is he there?"

"Look, Daymion, I know that I should have said something to you, but I knew you wouldn't agree with my plan. I did what I thought would work."

"And so, what happened to watching the house and planning a move on it?"

"I spooked Kenny when I ran in on him. When I went back, he was gone and so was everything else. I haven't seen him or Shay since."

"So now, we're just living on hope that they will turn up and a prayer that my son is safe out there?"

"He's safe, Daymion. I've been keeping post. You know I'm not going to let anything happen to him."

Daymion grew silent. He had yet to be able to spend some time with Dre. The few times he had been around only turned into a disagreement of some sort. Kayla had warned him about trying to run Dre's life, when he had never been a part of it. The last thing Daymion wanted to do was push his son away from him, so in order to keep him close, the best thing for him to do was go along with whatever he chose. Afterall, he trusted Mellow with his own life so he knew he could trust him with Dre's.

"I don't mean to be so angry towards you, but Mellow, you and I both know what the streets lead to and it's not a pretty picture. Ain't shit out there good for none of us and I just don't want Dre to fall victim to it. His life has been rough enough without it."

"I know what Dre's been through. I was there, Daymion. That boy was living a grown man's life before he was even grown enough to do it, but he made it through, and he's going to make it again. I know it's not what you want, but it's what he was born to do, whether you like it or not. He knows how to handle his business out there and I ain't never far from him."

Daymion knew Mellow was telling the truth, but even knowing he was out there looking out for Dre, it still didn't ease his mind. However, he would let Mellow continue on with whatever he had planned. He trusted him completely.

"Look, Mell, I have to leave town for a few days on some business, but I need to know that you gone be okay with it."

"Come on now, Day. You know I got this. I ain't neva let you down before so stop tripping and asking questions you already know the answer to."

"Thanks. And when I get back, we gonna throw a little get together for Dre. Do some barbequin' and shit like that."

"That's straight. Lil nigga'll like that. Make him realize he got people that care about him now. Maybe it will stop him from being so damn angry."

"Nah, that's his momma's fault, but she ain't here to make it right so he's going to always carry that with him."

Mellow thought for a moment before he asked his next question. He didn't want to offend anyone, but he was curious and wanted an answer! He just hoped Daymion would give him one.

"Yo, Day, I know how Kiara did ya boy and it wasn't very sweet. Why he ain't shaking Malachi's hand instead of trying to take him out? And I guess I should be wondering the same thing about you?"

"Don't matter how she did him. She's still his mother and can't shit change that. Dre knows the honorable thing to do is avenge her and as for me, I'm doing it out of respect for my boy. I also got a prior beef with Malachi. One that we never had a chance to resolve."

"Oh yeah? You ain't never told me that. How did it come about?"

"I killed Shay's mother, but it was an accident. It wasn't her I was aiming for. She had been fucking with Dory while he was running for me. His ass woke up one day and decided he was going to be my competition. Shit became a small gun war between us, but he fired first. I caught him off guard one day when he was out with Malia and took a shot. When he realized I had pulled the trigger, he grabbed her and used her as a shield. Bullet struck her right in the throat. She was pregnant with Malalchi's son at the time, and I guess you could probably figure the rest out for yourself."

"Damn, so Dory was always a pussy. I knew it. And now, I see why Malachi treated Dre like shit on the bottom of his shoes. He was on some get back."

"Yeah, and this drama has gone on between us all this time. Had I not got locked up fucking with Kiara's ass, we would have been faced off. I'm the reason he treated her the way he did, even though she probably did deserve it too. Our beef will only end when one of us is in the ground. I'd prefer it to be him, but to save De, I'd rather it be me.

"Don't worry, Day, we gone get his ass. Fuck putting him six feet. We gonna put his evil ass down ten deep."

The two of them shared a laugh and gave each other dap. They talked a little while longer and then Mellow finally left. When he was gone, Daymion sat back and thought about his days with Kiara. He had to admit, shit was sweet until he found out her real age. He could still remember her sassy but confident attitude. Kiara knew she had it going on with her pretty face, slim waist and fat ass. Her fun, silly ways kept him entertained and he enjoyed the intelligent conversations the two of them shared. Everything in their world had been going great until the day Daymion found out about her age. He often wondered how a fifteen-year-old had so much sexual experience. Kiara had deep-throated his dick and fucked him like she was a grown ass woman. There was no way he could have ever guessed she was so young and wished she would have just been honest with him from the jump. It was too late to worry about it though, because the shit was done and over with.

Daymion finally pushed Kiara from his mental and thought about the trip he had to make. Kayla had asked to go with him, but he needed her on standby just in case shit didn't go as planned. Daymion had been turned on to a dealer named Hector out of Texas who got his supply straight from the cocoa fields in Mexico. Daymion's old connect, Julio, had been diagnosed with lung cancer and was in his final stages. He wanted to make sure Daymion was hooked up before he succumbed to his illness. Julio had been close friends with Hector's parents and had raised him to be the man he was. Hector's mother died of a drug overdose when he was only six years old and his father was stabbed to death while doing a bid in a Mexican prison. Hector had no one else, so Julio took him in.

Hector grew to be very successful in the drug game, and with Julio as his guide,he went to great heights. There was no one else Julio would rather Daymion deal with. He knew that Hector would do right by him and give him the same deals he did, plus Hector was low key with his business. Julio knew Daymion would be in good hands.

Daymion had been so deep in thought that he didn't even hear Kayla walk into the room, but her presence was always welcome no matter what frame of mind he was in.

"Hey, you. How did it go with Mellow? I hope you wasn't too hard on him."

"You know me too well. I did go in hard at first, but I softened up. I know he would never put Dre in a position he couldn't get him out of, but I still have to worry. It's part of my job.

"Don't worry, Daymion. Everything is going to work out just the way you want it to. It always does."

"Oh yeah? Well, why don't you follow me upstairs to our bedroom so I can test that theory?"

"Now why do we have to go all the way up there when right here is perfectly fine?"

Kayla smiled and walked over to the cabinet that housed Daymion's CD player. She put in a "Vedo" disc and went straight to Daymion's favorite track.

Can you wear that perfume that I like? Oh yea. Can you wear that satin dress? Uh huh, Baby, then let down your hair. Can I have you just the way I like? Right there. Can I lay you on the bed? Run my fingers through your hair? Your legs, right there. My hands, right here. My lips, your ear. As I whisper, 'bout to enter. Your hips my gip, you bite your lip. From down under, feel that thunder. I can hear your rivers flow, feigning possibilities. I can feel it, water drippin'. It's clouding my mental and we might not make it to my bed. Can we pull over? Right there, I don't care who's there. Baby, can we pull over?"

While the words to *Pull Over* filled the room, Kayla turned around and swayed her hips. Slowly, she stripped to the beat. Daymion loved it when she got freaky and did shit like that. She kept things in their relationship interesting and never slacked when it came to keeping his attention and he knew it would always be that way.

Once Kayla was completely nude, she walked over to Daymion and grabbed his hand. As soon as she sucked one of his fingers into her mouth, he stood and picked her up. Kayla wrapped her legs around his waist as he carried her to his desk. He laid her on the hundred dollar bills he had been counting before Mellow showed up. He needed to be inside of the woman he loved, and he couldn't wait another minute. Daymion spread her thighs, dropped his pants and went to work.

Kayla was his heaven on earth and the peace she brought him couldn't compare to anything else. Mellow had become like a brother to him and as soon as he could make a connection with Dre, he felt like his life would finally be solid, but little did he know, his world was about to crumble.

Chapter 14

Dre could still smell Shay's scent on his clothing as he put his key in the lock. He wasn't sure what to expect once he walked through the door, but he was almost certain that it was going to be bad. He knew he should have gone straight home when he left the block, but running into Shay had been unexpected. Dre didn't even think twice when she asked him to take a ride with her and even though he knew it was wrong, he didn't object to going to a hotel. He hadn't planned to stay out all night, but one thing had led to another, and the next thing he knew, it was daylight. Thankfully, Tasha wasn't the type of bitch to blow up his phone. She would rather sit back and wait on him to show and then confront him face to face.

Dre opened the door slowly, just in case she tried to run up on him. He was surprised when he walked inside and she was nowhere to be seen, at least as far as he could tell. Dre shut the door behind him and walked further inside. It was the middle of the day but inside the walls of the house seemed dark and dreary. The silence was fucking with Dre's mind, but he continued to walk through it. He really didn't want to hear Tasha bitching, but the quiet space was too much for him to take. He finally heard her voice when he walked into the living room.

"How dare you come back home to me smelling like that bitch? And don't tell me that I'm tripping because I know you were with her."

"Tasha, come on. It ain't what you thinking. Just give me a chance to explain."

Dre walked up closer to the couch where Tasha was sitting with a blanket wrapped around her. The pillow that lay on the end of the couch told him that was where she had slept in anticipation of him coming home. All the blinds had been closed, making the room dim, but there was still enough light for Dre to see the hurt in her eyes. He knew that Tasha deserved nothing but the truth, but the only thing he could get out was lies.

"Oh yeah, Dre, it's exactly what I'm thinking. You could have at least had the decency to wash up and get her stank ass smell off of you."

"It wasn't necessary, Tasha, because ain't shit happen between us. We just talked, that's all. There was a lot of shit we needed to get off our chest."

"Do you really think I'm that dumb, Dre? Why can't you just stand up and keep that shit real? Don't I deserve that much from you?"

"Look, I don't have time to stand here and listen to you bitch about something you don't know a damn thing about. I'ma go take me a shower and lie down so I can get some sleep."

Dre turned around and walked away, but Tasha was right on his tracks. She didn't take disrespect kindly, especially, up in her own house. She followed Dre all the way to the bedroom with an attitude that was warranted. When he opened the bedroom door and saw his stuff sitting in a box by the bed, he stopped and turned around. Tasha stood with her hands on her hips and that look of hurt still in her eyes.

"The fuck is all this, Tasha?"

"It's the little bit of shit you own, and you need to get it out of my house."

"Oh, so we gonna play that game? Where the fuck am I supposed to go?"

"Go stay with that bitch or ya daddy. I don't give a damn which one, but you getting the hell out of here. Dre, please. Just get your stuff and go. And make sure you give me my key before you walk out because your ass ain't welcome here no more."

Tasha left the bedroom in tears. She couldn't believe that he found it so easy to lie to her after all she had been through with him. She had fought for so long to be number one in his life, but she just didn't make the cut. All she wanted Dre to do was leave before she changed her mind. As much as she loved him, she had to let him go. At least for the time being, because as long as she allowed him to continue to do her any kind of way, he would think it was okay. Tasha's grandmother raised her better than that. She deserved to be loved by a man who only looked at her and until Dre could do that, he had to go.

Dre shook his head and walked over to the box. He sat on the bed beside it and then looked around the room. He knew he had fucked up, but he didn't know what to do about it. Dre knew that he couldn't run back to Shay, because honestly, he didn't even know where to find her. He had been so caught up in his feelings that he forgot to ask how to get in touch with her, but she hadn't bothered to offer the information either.

The last thing Dre wanted to do was go to his father's house, but he really didn't have any other options. He let out a long sigh and called himself a taxi. He didn't want to leave, but he felt it was best to give Tasha some space. He hoped she wouldn't call his father and tell him what had happened because Daymion would be pissed if he found out Dre had hooked up with Shay and let her walk away without getting information on Malachi. He knew that Tasha had never been the messy type, but he had to remember that she was in her feelings and was liable to do anything.

Dre picked up the box that held the little bit of stuff he had accumulated since being home and walked out of the bedroom. Tasha stood at the front door with her hand held out and when Dre reached in his pocket and pulled out the house key, she took it and walked off. Dre shook his head and walked out the front door to the awaiting taxi. He looked back at the house one more time and got in. he couldn't believe that he had fucked up already, but it was too late to take back what he had done. He didn't know why Shay had such a tight grip on him, but he had to somehow get out of it. Hurting Tasha had never been his intention and somehow, he would make it right. He just needed to figure things out.

Dre breathed a sigh of relief when he noticed Daymion's car gone. It would give him a little bit of time to get his story together because he felt like he would need one. When Kayla opened the door, Dre walked in and sat his box down. Kayla wasn't the kind of woman to ask questions because she felt that she didn't have to, and she was right.

"Hey, auntie Kayla. I guess you can tell by the box I need a place to stay. I just don't know for how long."

"Dre, you know you are always welcome here, and your timing couldn't be better because Daymion is out of town for a few days."

"Well, that gives me some relief. I mean, I know I haven't spent a lot of time with him since I been out and that may seem wrong to everybody else, but I ain't had him all my life. As bad as I'd like to bond and build something solid with pops, I can't just run into it like that. I got to take my time and ease myself into it because I don't have room for any more disappointment."

"I can understand that, Dre. I know firsthand what you've been through, and it may not seem like it, but Daymion is a patient man and he'll be there when you're ready. In the meantime, what's going on with you and that box?"

Kayla pointed to the box and crossed her arms over her chest. Dre was still young, and yet, he had so much drama in his life. Somehow, it just seemed to follow him everywhere he went.

"I fucked up and Tasha put my ass out."

"That was quick, but what could you have possibly done to cause something that serious?"

Dre cut his eyes away from Kayla and looked down. She knew that look all too well because she had seen it more times then she'd like to remember. She could never understand why men went astray when they had good women at home. As far as she knew, Daymion had kept it real, and she did everything in her power to make sure it stayed that way.

"I ran into Shay on the block, and instead of going home like I should have done, I went with her. I guess I don't need to tell you what happened after that."

"Dre, why would you do that to her? Tasha rode hard for you while you were locked up and you should be appreciating her, not pushing her to the side for a nothing ass bitch like Shay. I'm very disappointed by your actions, but what's done is done. Give Tasha some time and talk to her but only if you're going to have the right intentions.

"I know I fucked up, but I'ma figure out how to make it right. For now, though, I need to handle some business on the block, but I have one problem. I need some wheels. Think you could help me out?"

Kayla didn't even hesitate. She walked over to her purse and pulled out her car keys, handing them right to Dre. She trusted that he would take care of the Benz as if it was his own, because there was no way she could save him from Daymion if he didn't. Daymion had offered to buy Dre his own ride. He told him he could have any car he wanted, no matter the price, but Dre turned him down because he didn't want to be in anybody's debt. Kayla hated the fact that Dre felt like he couldn't completely depend on Daymion, but she understood why. Having to grow up without him had been hard on Dre, but thankfully even though Kiara raised him on her own, he still turned out just fine. Kayla still remembered the day Dre asked her to take him to meet Daymion. He had been so anxious to have him in his life, but it seemed as if he'd had a change of heart because Dre avoided Daymion as much as he possibly could.

When Dre started Kayla's Benz, the engine purred to life with ease. He decided that when he got his own ride, he would also get a Benz. Dre already had it picked out in his mind. A big body Benz, money green with gold trim sitting on twenty twos. An all-wood range and a stereo system that other niggas would envy. But first, he had to make sure Malachi got taken care of. Once he killed him, the Benz would be a reward. A gift to himself.

Dre drove from block to block for almost an hour in hopes of seeing Shay's ride somewhere, but he had no luck. He was about to head back so he could return Kayla's ride but changed his mind. He figured that since he was already out, he might as well post up and put in a little work. Dre made sure to park Kayla's ride out of sight, but still close enough for him to get to just in case he needed a quick getaway.

For the next couple of hours, the fiends came and went. Some with small bills, others with big faces. Dre had never cared what amount they came to him with because all money spent the same. He thought back to when he first hit the block. Dre had been scared as hell, but he didn't show it, and no matter how many times Malice came at him, he continued to push on. He had gone out there for his momma because he wanted to make her happy, but he now realized that nothing would have changed how she felt about him and nothing she did could change how he felt about her.

Dre loved his momma, but for some reason, he never told her. He wondered if telling her would have made a difference because, deep down, he felt like love was all she needed. Not the kind she had gotten from Malachi because his kind wasn't genuine, but the kind that only a son could give her. Dre knew that it was too late to tell the woman who gave him life what she needed to hear. Avenging her murder seemed to be the only way for Dre to make it up to her and he wouldn't stop until he did just that.

Dre had been so deep in his own mind that he didn't see Kenny walk up on him. It was only when Kenny spoke that Dre snapped out of it.

"So, I see you back out here at it, huh? Thought you would have had enough of this shit, especially when yo ass got jacked."

"Oh, so you recognize me tonight, because if I remember correctly, the last time you came this way, you were so high off that shit you ain't know who I was."

"Nigga, I don't even know what you talking about because I don't fuck off like that. You gots to be trippin'."

"Yeah? Well, I guess I was also tripping when I hit the hotel with Shay for the night."

"Whatever, but Shay my bitch now and she would never betray me like that. She been told me that she ain't want nothing to do with you. Whatever you thought y'all had ain't no more so get over it."

"That's what she said? Because this dick had her saying something totally different."

Dre could tell that Kenny wasn't sure if he should believe him or not. Kenny had to know that he was only a substitute for what Shay really wanted and even though Dre spent that night with her he knew he would never do it again. Shay had gone behind his back and fucked his partner and because of that Dre couldn't trust her completely. He hated the fact that he had fucked things up with Tasha but after he took care of Malachi, he planned on making it up to her.

"You lucky we out in public because you 'pose to have a slug in your dome for that disrespect."

"Don't let being out here stop you because I'm ready for whatever. Keep in mind though, I'm not that same mufucka I was back in the day, so when you bring me some heat, just know, you the one that's gone get burned."

"It's all good and I'ma let you have that, but make sure you watch your back because you don't ever know where I'll be. Oh yeah, tell my lil sis I said what's up."

Kenny smirked and walked away because honestly, he hadn't gone there to start any drama. He always felt like he needed to be on the defensive when it came to Dre, because, in a way, he still felt guilty about all he had done to him. Dre had always kept shit real between them and looked out for Kenny every time he came up on something and still, Kenny stabbed him in the back. His pride stood in the way of mending anything that had gone down between them.

Dre wasn't too worried about Kenny because he had always been a pussy. Yeah, he had got him for his cash and his bitch, but he would never be man enough to get him for his life no matter how hard he tried.

Dre looked down at his watch, a plain black digital Casio because he wasn't trying to be flashy and noticed how late it had gotten. He was certain that Kayla would be worried, not only about her ride but about him too. The last thing he wanted to do was upset her. She had been the one constant in his life, and he loved her as if she were his own mother. He just hoped she knew it. He thought he should let her know, just in case.

Dre looked around to make sure no more sales were coming his way. At first, he had only agreed to go back out on the block in hopes of bringing Malachi out of hiding, but his frame of mind had changed. He got an adrenaline rush from being out there, plus, he liked how fat his pockets had grown. Dre never wanted to depend on others so having his own cash was important to him. He felt like once he got rid of Malachi, he would push himself even more and raise his status.

Dre put one foot in front of the other and proceeded to walk to where he parked the Benz. He was thankful that the mosquitos hadn't been that bad because he hated the smell of insect repellant, plus, it was too warm out for long sleeves.

Dre was almost to Kayla's ride when he pulled the keys out of his pocket. Nothing but silence surrounded him until he heard a gunshot. Dre didn't have a weapon on him, but he reached for one out of habit. Before he could turn around to see where the shot had come from, his body hit the ground.

Chapter 15

Dre didn't know it, but Mellow had sat out on the block and watched him work every night since he had been out there. He knew Dre had never been fond of the grind, but he was a natural at it, and the dope fiends flocked to him like flies on a pile of shit. Dre was a go-getter in his own special way, but the fact that he was Daymion Myers' son gave him an advantage over everyone else. The hood respected and looked up to Daymion, therefore, they would do the same with Dre.

Mellow had admired the young up and comer ever since that first day Dre stepped foot inside Dory's crib. Mellow had always been good at reading people and as soon as he looked Dre in the eyes, he could see the hurt and anger he had hidden inside, and yet, Dre stood strong like a soldier. After Mellow learned about all Dre had gone through, he admired him that much more, because most mufuckas would have grown cold and bitter. Mellow knew because although, he followed God, he was one of them mufuckas.

When Mellow was growing up, his mother took him to church every Sunday and WEdnesday, but on all other days, he was left to fend for himself while his mother, who was a drug addict, turned tricks. He could still remember there being a constant flow of men in and out of their home, a lot of them from the very church they attended. None of those men ever claimed to be his father, but he always hoped and prayed to God that one would step up and rescue him from the situation he was in.

With the exception of those men, his mother had been good at hiding who she truly was. Mellow went to bed hungry almost every night. He would lay in his bed and read his bible in hopes of getting some fulfillment. Those times that his mother couldn't get a fix, she would lash out and punch or kick him, and then ask him to forgive her. Mellow would often leave and walk around the block for hours just to avoid going back home. He would wait until he thought she was asleep before going back home.

Mellow had begun to grow angry and withdrawn because he needed something to replace the hurt and pain he held in his heart. He had to get on his knees and pray to God to remove the visions he had of going in her room and slitting his mother's throat. Thankfully, his mother smoked so much crack one night, she ended up having a massive heart attack. Mellow tried, but he couldn't find the strength to mourn her. The woman who had birthed him meant nothing to him. Mellow even refused to attend her funeral.

After his mother's death, Mellow moved in with the pastor and his wife and even though he stayed in the church, he still moped around in the streets night after night. Finally, one of the local dealers approached him and gave him a small package to sell. At first, Mellow wasn't feeling the sin he was committing but once his pockets began to fill with cash, his whole attitude changed. He figured he could serve God and still do the devil's work. His guilt would often eat him up inside, but he pressed on because he had an image to uphold.

When Mellow would be out on the block, he was cool with the niggas that were on that pipe, but he gave the females a hard time. Each one of them reminded him of his mother so he would talk to them with disrespect and treat them like shit, when one of them propositioned him, he made her suck his dick in front of all the other dealers. He did one crack fiend so dirty she ended up committing suicide. After that, Mellow had a reawakening and asked God to change his ways. Now when he looked back, he felt deep remorse for what he had done.

Mellow felt like his job was to look out for Dre, because he reminded him so much of himself. He didn't want Dre to fall into the same pits he himself had been in, even though he was the one who had suggested Dre being out there. Mellow wanted Malachi just as bad as Daymion, because a mufucka like him didn't deserve to breathe the same air as good people did. Mellow never understood how Dre managed to keep his mental together, but if something happened that caused Dre to lose it, Mellow would be there. He had love for Dre and deep inside the depths of his hardened heart, he had love for his mother too.

Mellow leaned back in his seat but made sure he could still keep an eye on Dre. he said a silent prayer for Dre and for his enemies and then pushed play on Bryann T's newest disc. Mellow closed his eyes and listened as "I choose Love" poured from his speakers. "Counterfeit friendships, snakes that give you handshakes. Look at the eye contact and the face your man makes. Devil is grand plotting, evil on your downfall. Follow you home, then later, come make a house call. Never been cleansed by the love of God, so he evil though, but King Tut ain't got nothin' on my King Jesus though, I know you selfish, shady, shiesty and sneaky. I know you hate me, it's in your eyes when you see me. I gotta love you regardless, it ain't easy. I won't allow Satan's darkness, just to defeat me. I try my best to bring peace as much as possible. It can be peaceful between us, I think it's possible. I get frustrated and angry sometimes. I'm human, bruh. Just understand, I won't let my anger consume me. If I can forgive the ones who killed my brother, for real. I can forgive whoever, so hatred can disappear."

Mellow was bobbing his head to the beat when he felt something shift inside of him. He opened his eyes and looked straight at Dre, who stood there without a care in the world. Mellow looked from side to side and even behind him, but nothing seemed out of the ordinary. However, something was still off. The empty glances didn't seem right to him, so he got out of his ride and shut the door quietly. He stood as still as he could and looked toward Dre again.

Mellow thought he was trippin' and chuckled to himself. He had never been a paranoid nigga so he couldn't understand why he was feeling that way. His eyes were telling him one thing while his gut was telling him something else. Mellow knew he would never be able to live with himself if something happened to Dre, so that was why he stayed on post watching over him. Mellow shook his head and was about to get back in his ride when he saw movement from the corner of his eye.

Mellow turned his head in time to see the man pull a weapon from his waistband. He tried to see if he could identify the culprit, but the hoodie the man wore obscured his view. Mellow watched closely as the man raised the gun and pointed it, and then he followed the direction it was pointed in. The man had his finger on the trigger ready to fire, but the hoodie slipped off his head stopping him. The man quickly pulled his hoodie back up, but it was down long enough for Mellow to get a good look at him.

Mellow couldn't believe his luck. He wanted to pick up his phone and call Daymion, but he knew it would be pointless because Daymion had gone out of town and wouldn't be able to show up anyway. Mellow would have to handle the situation on his own and he would have to move at the right pace because he didn't have a lot of time to spare, like it or not, he knew what he had to do, and he was ready.

Mellow put his palms together and sent a quick prayer up to the God he believed in. He repented for his sins and asked for forgiveness for all the things he had done. He found the need to apologize to God for being ashamed to show others who he really was. Mellow knew he should have chosen the right path, but he felt like if he wouldn't have chosen the one he was on, he wouldn't be where he was at the time he needed to be there. He wondered if that had been his purpose all along. Mellow had hoped to one day be a father and raise a Christian son, but looking out for Dre may have been as close as he would ever get to being one.

After Mellow said his prayer, a sense of peace fell over him. It was time to make a sacrifice, the same way Christ had done for him. Mellow held up a peace sign toward the sky and took off running. It was his moment, and he wanted to be remembered as a soldier, not seen as a coward.

As soon as Mellow made contact with Dre, he felt the bullet penetrate his neck. One single shot opened him right up. Suddenly, everything grew quiet except for the ringing in his ears. Mellow felt movement and the next thing he knew he was looking up into Dre's eyes.

"Mellow, what the hell did you do that for? Are you fucking crazy?"

"It-It was, was you or me, and-and your pops depended on me to make sure you-you-you were safe. I-I-I kn-know I convinced you to g-g-go back out in these streets, but-but ch-ch-choose another path. This ain't the life f-f-for you."

"I will, Mellow. I will, but you gotta hold on. Mufucka, you can't die on me. Me and pops need you. You can't leave us yet."

The sounds of sirens could be heard in the distance, and as Mellow lay there in Dre's arms dying, his concern wasn't on himself. Mellow felt like Dre didn't deserve to be punished any more than he already had. Mellow had made Daymion a promise and there was no way he would break it.

"Go on, Dre, get out of here and go make shit real with your pops. That nigga love you, and he gone need you. This right here, it's, it's gone be it for me. God opened those cemetery gates just, just for me so I gotta go. My-My-My work here is done."

"Mellow, what the hell are you talking about? You trippin' and I can't leave you like this. t ain't right."

"It's okay. This is how it's supposed to be. This why G, god put, put me in your life. I did what, what he put me here to do, but now I gotta rest, and because of you, I, I can rest in peace."

"What does all that even mean? Shit, shit, shit, what the hell am I supposed to tell pops?"

"Tell-Tell him. It was Malachi."

As soon as Mellow said the name, his eyes closed permanently. Time was up for him and since he had lived the best life he could, he had been ready. Dre felt the tears well up in his eyes as he held Mellows limp body close to him. He didn't want to leave him there like a piece of garbage, but the sounds of the sirens made him rethink his options. Dre looked down at mellow one last time and then laid him on the ground.

Dre stood and looked around, but the streets were empty. It seemed strange to him but he didn't have time to stand there and dwell on it. He looked down and saw that his clothes were covered in blood but there was nothing he could do about it, at least not yet. He had drugs and drug money on him and not to mention, a dead man's blood. Dre knew he had to get the hell outta dodge before the men in blue got there. He wasn't about to catch another case and spend the rest of his life inside of a prison cell. Dre had too much other shit he had to take care of and he had to be free to do it.

Dre took off and ran to Kayla's ride. He opened the door and quickly got inside, but as soon as he tried to push the key into the ignition, his hand shook. Wasn't a mufucka on earth that put fear in his heart, so he knew it wasn't because he was afraid. Dre shook out of hurt and anger. Malachi Jensen had taken out someone else he cared about, and Dre swore it would be the last one. That bastard had to pay.

Dre was well aware of the fact that the bullet was meant for him but Mellow stepped in and changed its fate. Only real mufuckas did shit like that and Mellow was the realest nigga he had ever known. Dre knew that Mellow's death would hit Daymion in the worst way because he looked at Mellow like his own flesh and blood. They were like brothers and had a bond as solid as steel.

Dre put his foot on the gas and drove away from the block as carefully as he could. He couldn't afford to be seen by anyone, especially Malachi, who he hoped had already left. Dre suddenly felt guilt seep into his heart, because if it wouldn't have been for him, Mellow wouldn't have been out there in the first place. Dre didn't even have a clue that Mellow would be out watching over him like that, and although he was grateful to be alive, he wished somehow Mellow could have been spared.

Tears stung Dre's eyes and blurred his vision, but he somehow still managed to make it safely to his destination. He knew he would have to step up and be there for his father, but first, he needed someone to be there for him. Dre pulled up in front of Tasha's house and killed the engine. He wasn't even sure if she'd welcome him, but he needed her. Yeah, what he did with Shay was real fucked up, but at the end of the day, he knew it was Tasha who had him. She had always had him and he would one day repay her for her loyalty.

Dre got out and walked to her front door. He stood and stared at it a couple of minutes before he finally rang the bell. Tasha was a lady, and even though she pushed drugs for his father, she didn't hang in the streets heavy like that. He knew that she was inside trying to fall asleep with a heart he had broken into pieces. He wouldn't fault her if she turned him away, but Dre knew real bitches did real things.

Tasha opened the door and said nothing. She just stood there and stared at Dre through empty, emotionless eyes. Dre said nothing either, because he felt like he was choking on his own pain. Tasha looked at Dre real good and as soon as she noticed the blood all over his clothes, she turned into the woman he knew he didn't deserve. He had hurt her and yet, she pushed her pain to the side so she could comfort him through his.

Dre didn't appear to have any wounds, so Tasha knew the blood had to belong to someone else. She wasn't about to ask any questions, because the less she knew, the better off she would be. If Dre wanted to tell her, it would be up to him. All she wanted to do was get him cleaned up and into some fresh clothes. When she had put him out, she had put some of his stuff to the side just to give him a reason to come back, but she never would have guessed he would show up the way that he had.

"Come on, Dre. Let's go get you cleaned up and into something fresh. You can't stay like this."

"Don't you wanna know what happened? I mean, I'm covered in blood and you ain't asked me shit."

"What you do out there in them streets is your business, and the last thing you need is me as a co-defendant. I see that you're not hurt, so nothing else matters."

Dre respected her answer and remembered just how thorough Tasha was. What she didn't know couldn't be used against her, but he needed her to know what he was going through and what he was up against. His enemy had stuck and missed. Dre just hoped when he returned fire, he wouldn't.

After getting cleaned up, Dre tried to put something in his stomach, but he just couldn't build up an appetite, so he decided to lie down with Tasha close by his side. Dre stared at the ceiling because every time closed his eyes, he saw visions of Mellow's lifeless body lying in his arms. As soon as the first tear rolled down his cheek, he told Tasha what happened.

"Mellow. That nigga saved my life. That was his blood on me, blood that was supposed to be mine. He gave his last breath just so my lungs could go on pumping. Mellow took a hit that was meant for me and now he's gone and he ain't never coming back. That shits on me, because I was the reason he was there."

"No, Dre, no. You can't put that on you, and Mellow would be pissed if he knew that you were doing it. He knows you would have done the same thing for him, so you cannot eat that blame. And does your father know what happened, because Mellow was his best friend."

"Nah. Pops out of town so he don't know shit. I gotta make that call because I feel like he should hear it straight from me. Pops ain't gone have no mufuckin' understanding because he told Mellow not to put my ass out there in the first place. He told me to keep my black ass out them streets and I ain't listen. Now look what the fuck done happened."

"It's going to be alright, Dre. I know that Daymion is going to be hurt behind this, but at least he still has you."

"Yeah? Let's just hope that's enough."

It took hours for Dre to finally fall asleep, but once he did, he slept hard. He needed the rest because he knew once Daymion found out about Mellow, the hunt for Malachi would go full force, and nobody was going to get any rest until he was zipped up in a body bag.

Chapter 16

Finding out about Mellow's murder hit too close to home for Daymion, and made him feel like he was living his brother's death all over again. Somehow, Mellow had come into his life and filled the void that Trey had left behind. Daymion had depended on Mellow for everything and he couldn't believe that his right hand was gone. Kayla couldn't even comfort him the way she usually did.

They say a death brings people closer and for Daymion and Dre, those words rang true. Both of them had their own special ties to Mellow, and in the end, losing him made their bond stronger. Together, they would make sure Malachi regretted what he had done. Mellow didn't deserve to die, but had he not given his life, it would have been Dre gone instead. Everybody knew who the bullet was meant for, but being the real nigga Mellow was, he jumped in the way and took it like a soldier.

Daymion went all out and spared no expense on Mellow's homegoing. He ordered everyone who attended to wear all white as a sign of peace and unity, which was all Mellow ever wanted to bring to the hood. Bryann T's music played in the background as people took turns and walked up one by one to the casket to pay their respect. Daymion stood by and watched each one of them closely. He knew some of them were there just to make sure Mellow was really dead. Mellow never really had enemies, but he had haters by the dozen, which was only a part of the game.

The funeral lasted a couple of hours and went without any problems. After it ended, everyone proceeded to the cemetery and threw hundred-dollar bills on the casket as it was lowered into the earth. Daymion, of course, furnished those bills but told all the people that they were counterfeit in hopes to sway them from taking the money.

Daymion made sure the cemetery was surrounded with armed men. He couldn't take any chances and since he would be distracted by the event, he needed someone to have his back. Once Mellow was lowered into the ground, all the people began to clear out. They would forget Mellow in a couple of days and move on with their lives, but there was no way Daymion would ever be able to move past it. He would forever carry the memories with him. He had even gone and got Mellow's portrait tattooed on the right side of his chest, opposite of Trey's. Since both of them shared a piece of his heart, he felt like that was where they belonged.

Kayla walked up behind Daymion and stood there quietly for a moment. She knew there was nothing she could say or do to ease what he was feeling, so she wasn't going to even try. She had lost ones that were close to her too, so she understood exactly what he was going through.

Kayla finally got closer and put her arms around his waist. She lightly squeezed him just to let him know that she would always be there for him. She held on to him for only a few minutes and then let him go. Kayla knew he needed a little time, so she walked away and left him to his feelings. As soon as she was out of sight, one of Mellows block boys approached him.

"Sup, Daymion? I just wanted to check on you because I know this shit hit you harder than anyone. So, you aiight?"

Daymion scrunched his eyebrows and gave him a look as if he was telling him that he had some nerve to even speak to him. The nigga might have worked for Mellow, but he didn't know shit about Daymion. If he had, he would have known better than to approach him in the first place.

"Do I look like I'm alright to you? The fuck is you supposed to be anyway?"

"Names Jason, and I ain't mean no disrespect or anything like that. I was just checking up on you, bruh, that's all. The whole crew knew what type of brotherhood you and Mellow had and you can play hard all you want, but a nigga like me done lost before, and when I did, I needed me a mufucka to step up and make sure I was aiight. Guess what? Nobody gave a fuck, so it only made the shit harder to deal with. I'm only here right now trying to be to you the person I needed myself. If you can't handle that, then fuck it. I'll be on my way, and you can stay here and drown in your sorrow by your fuckin' self."

Daymion was shocked at Jason's boldness, and he had to give the nigga credit for even taking the chance of stepping to him at all. For that, Daymion decided to find out what the nigga was about, so when Jason turned to walk away, Daymion stopped him. "You said your name was Jason, but you ain't say what you about or how you can benefit me."

Jason stopped and slowly turned around to face Daymion again. He knew it would be his only opportunity, so he had to make the best of it. "Look, I know ain't no mufucka around that can replace Mellow, but I'd like to give it a shot, if possible. I mean, you eventually gone need a backup plan and I'm all about that paper chasin'. I'm also a master at gunplay. Been shooting mufuckas since I was a git. Half of 'em never even did shit to me, I just felt like pulling the trigger on 'em. It's a miracle that I'm even standing in front of you right now because I should have done been took out. Guess God ain't got a place for me yet."

Daymion stood and stared at Jason for a minute, so he could take in all he had said. He had to admit, the nigga had some heart, and in some crazy way, reminded him of Mellow. He wondered if Jason would be willing to risk his own life the same way, but before he had a chance to ask him, Dre walked up. Daymion said nothing, but Jason somehow knew that it was time for him to leave. He just hoped that when he did, he didn't become just a memory because he needed that work. Now that Mellow was gone, he needed to make sure he had a secure spot somewhere on the set. Jason's mother was dying from an AIDS-related illness, but he wanted her to be as comfortable as she could until she took her last breath. In order for that to happen, Jason had to make sure her medication never ran out and the meds were very expensive, so Jason was willing to do anything to keep them coming.

Dre waited until Jason was out of earshot before he spoke. He had a lot of shit built up inside and he felt like he needed to get it off his chest. It may not have been the best time, but Dre felt like it was the right time. Mellow had asked him to make things good with Daymion and that was exactly what he planned to do.

"Ya know, pops, I been angry for a long time. Angry at you. When I was growing up, I ain't have no one that I could depend on or that I could look up to. No one was there to teach me how to be a man. The only person there was my momma, and honestly, she ain't give a fuck if I lived or died. And even though, I had love for her, she made my heart cold as ice. I ain't give a damn about nothing. Since I been out, I been avoiding you because I felt like I couldn't be the son you needed me to be. That shits gone change, though. I ain't gone let past issues fuck up what I got today, and that's you pops."

"Dre, you are everything that I hoped you would be. No matter what has happened, that won't ever change. I'm proud of you and all that you have become, even after all your momma put you through. I give you my word, you ain't gone suffer again. Not as long as I have air in my lungs."

"Thanks, and all that playing hard shit I been doing, it's gonna stop. I'ma be right from now on. But we gotta take that mufucka out. This right here shouldn't have even happened, but I'ma take this one. Mellow's in that casket because of me. That's supposed to be me in there, pops, not him."

"No, Dre, it's not supposed to be you, and it shouldn't have been him either. But it's not on you, so let that blame go. And don't worry about Malachi. He's gone get his."

"You damn right he is."

Daymion and Dre turned to the voice and were shocked at who they saw. Kenny stood still because he wasn't sure what to expect from either one of them, but he knew it damn sure wouldn't be love. He had never personally done anything to Daymion, but he had fucked over Dre more times than he would like to remember. Dre didn't know it, but Kenny had come to try and squash the beef he had started between them.

Kenny had grown tired of the way he had been living and decided to make some big changes. Not only had he let the pipe go, but he had let Shay go too. He knew he never should have gotten involved with her, but the damage had been done and wasn't shit he could do to change that. If he could unfuck her, he would do it in a minute. He could tell by the look on Dre's face that he wasn't happy to see him, and he couldn't blame him at all. Daymion stood by and listened as the two of them exchanged words. He would only interfere if he had to, but he hoped it wouldn't come to that.

"Look, Dre. I know I'm the last person you want to see, but I'm here to make peace. I know that I done some fucked up shit to you and I'm sorry, but all I want is a chance to make it right."

"Oh yeah? Well making shit right would take you a hell of a long time. You sure you gone live long enough to make it all up?"

Kenny understood Dre's anger toward him, but he was determined to get his partner back. Kenny pulled the duffel bag from his shoulder and dropped it on the ground in front of him.

"That right there is all the money I took from you."

Dre looked at the bag but made no move to pick it up. He didn't trust Kenny. Too much damage had already been done and Dre wasn't sure it could be repaired. Kenny went to take a step forward and when he did, Dre pulled a gun. Dre had made sure to stay strapped at all times, especially after Mellow was killed. Kenny held his arms up in surrender just to let Dre know he hadn't come for gunplay.

"Shit ain't even got to come to that, Dre. I told you already that I come in peace. I know those years you spent away can't be given back, but there's your money. Every single dollar I took from you. And, Shay? I ain't fucking with her no more either. Never should have in the first place. I was dead ass wrong."

"And it took you all this time to realize that? The fuck did you do me like that for? Nigga, I ain't never did shit to you. I kept it one hundred at all times. You 'pose to do that kind of stuff to mufuckas who do you dirty. Not someone like me."

"I know, Dre, but what's done is done and ain't shit gone change that. All I know is that I want my partner back, and if at all possible, my sister, too."

Dre lowered his weapon as soon as Kenny mentioned his sister. Tasha was a rider, and yet, Dre himself had wronged her. However, when he needed her the most, she stood up for him. Kenny had never personally done anything to her, but she was mad at him for how he had done Dre. Kenny had also been ousted by the streets for his disloyalty, that was what enhanced his drug addiction. Dre felt bad because he had been abandoned all his life, making him feel like an outcast. There was no way he could do that to someone else.

"So, let's say I look past everything. How do I know you ain't gone turn and do the same shit again? And the fuck am I gone gain from letting it slide?"

Kenny looked from Dre to Daymion. He knew that however he responded would decide his fate. Kenny raised his eyebrows and smiled. He reached into his pocket very slowly because he didn't want them to think he was going for a weapon. Kenny saw Dre reach for his weapon again, but he didn't pull it, he was too busy staring at the cell phone Kenny had pulled out. Dre had a look of confusion on his face but Kenny cleared it up very quickly.

"I lead you to Malachi."

Chapter 17

Tasha sat back in the reclined seat and tried her best to relax her mind while the nail tech did wonders on her toes. Going to the spa and getting her nails done was on her list of favorite things to do because it not only made her feel special, but it gave her a break from all the bullshit that surrounded her.

Ever since Mellow's untimely death, Dre had not been himself, and it was driving Tasha crazy. He had become miserable to be around because the only thing he focused on was killing Malachi. He had even slacked in the bedroom and God knows Tasha needed some dick. She had been trying to sympathize with him, but she wasn't sure just how much longer she could do it. There were plenty of niggas that would have loved to get into Tasha's thongs, but she had never been a ho, and once she set her eyes on Dre, she never took them off of him.

Tasha had her eyes closed when she heard a voice she hadn't heard in a long time. At first, she thought she was tripping, but there was no denying the squeaky ass voice that irritated her down to her soul. Tasha opened her eyes and scrunched her nose up when she saw Shay with her hands on her hips drilling the nail tech. Tasha knew Shay wouldn't recognize her because she had never really been around any place she had been at, so Tasha zoned in and listened to what she was saying.

"Are you sure I didn't leave my phone here because I can't find it?"

"No, Miss Odom, I haven't seen your phone anywhere. You must have left it somewhere else."

"No, this was the last palace I was at before I went home, so it has to be here somewhere."

"Well, like I said, I haven't seen it, but you're more than welcome to look around. Just remember your boundaries. I have customers to tend to so do what you need to do."

The nail tech walked off and left Shay at the counter with an attitude. Tasha stared closely while Shay looked around the shop for her phone. Tasha almost wanted to laugh but she somehow managed to hold it in, and as bad as she wanted to get up and slap the bitch, the consequences of her actions stopped her. Tasha had never been ghetto, even though she was raised in one. Her grandma would have been so disappointed if she showed out in a public place, but it was taking everything inside of her to control herself. Tasha had been so focused on thinking about was to handle the bitch that she didn't even realize Shay was standing in front of her until she heard her voice again.

"You got a problem, bitch? Why the hell is you staring at me? I ain't into pussy."

Tasha looked up at the bitch who owned a piece of Dre's heart. She had a good mind to spit right in her face, but it would have been a waste of good saliva. Instead, Tasha put her feet to the floor and stood to face her competition. She had to give Shay credit; the bitch was pretty.

Shay's flawless images should have graced the covers of magazines. Tasha couldn't find one thing wrong with her skin and it made her sick on her stomach. She looked Shay up and down and could understand just how Dre got caught up. Everything about her was perfection and almost made Tasha sit back down. However, Tasha had never bowed down to a nigga and she'd be damned if she did it to a bitch.

"It ain't 'cause you a pretty bitch. I was actually just imagining all the ways I should beat your ass."

"You don't really want to do that and fuck up that fresh mani, now do you? I mean, I'm sure a broke bitch like you can't afford to get those all the time."

"I don't have to afford it, because my man makes sure I'm always good, unlike yours. While he's out there on that shit, you gotta fend for yourself. Now, let's talk about who can really afford something."

Tasha knew that Shay looked at her crazy because she wondered how she had that kind of information about her. Shay had always been a bougie bitch and for Tasha to put her business out there like that was an embarrassment. Shay hated the fact that her nigga was on that pipe because it made her look bad, but Tasha didn't give a damn about her feelings. She felt like Shay had already trampled all over hers for years, although, it was unknowingly, but Tasha was ready for some payback.

"Bitch, you don't know shit about me or my man, so go find you something else to play with. Something a little safer."

Shay turned to leave, but Tasha wasn't about to let her go so easily, she had a lot of built up tension in her chest and was ready to get rid of it, no matter what it cost her.

"Oh, I know you. You the bitch that keeps interfering in my life with Dre. You know that you don't mean him no good, and yet you won't stay your ass away so he can have a good life. A life where he ain't gotta worry about your fuck ass daddy taking out someone else he loves. Bitch, you already ruined my brother's life. I ain't gone let you ruin my man's, too."

"I don't know what the hell you're talking about because I've never interfered in Dre's life. He chooses to be with me so don't be mad when you taste my pussy on his lips."

The slap came so fast there was no way Shay could have avoided it. For a minute Tasha had forgotten where she was at, but the nail tech quickly reminded her.

"Excuse me, I don't know what's going on here, but I'm going to have to ask you two to leave. This is a place of business, and I can't afford to lose customers. Please, show some respect and go."

Shay looked at the lady with disgust, but Tasha wasn't about to blow her favorite spot. She picked up her Gucci bag and before walking out, reached inside of it and pulled out three crisp hundred dollar bills. She pressed them into the nail tech's palm and smiled.

"I'm so sorry for the disrespect, but here is a little something for your trouble."

The nail tech closed her fingers around the three bills and smiled. She quickly slid them inside her bra before she walked off to tend to another patron. Shay looked at Tasha and shook her head as if she pitied her. She would leave but she wasn't about to kiss ass and come out of her pocket when a bitch hadn't earned it. Shay turned to leave with Tasha close behind her. Tasha wasn't quite done with her yet, so once they made it outside, she went in.

"I don't know where you're going, bitch, because you are not off the hook. I owe you an ass whooping for all the shit me and Dre have went through because of you and your fuck ass father."

"What the hell are you talking about, and who the hell are you anyway?"

"Oh, so Kenny never mentioned his sister, huh? I forgot, he was too busy smoking that shit."

"Wait a minute, you're Tasha? Oh, I know all about you and your obsession with Dre. How you gone be mad at me? Dre is the one that you should be stepping to, because I don't owe you shit, and neither does my father."

Tasha had to admit, Shay was right because she didn't owe her a damn thing. Shay barely even knew Tasha and had never done anything personal to her. It was Dre that owed her the loyalty and respect, even though Tasha hated to admit it, she needed someone to blame, and Shay just seemed like the right fit. Tasha was tired of the drama and had decided that the fighting for Dre's affection was over. If he didn't want her, she would move on and let Shay or whoever else have him.

"You know what, Shay? You right, you don't owe me shit. I've been mad at you for years. From the first day I heard your name come out of Dres' mouth, I hated you. I had no reasoning for how I felt, but as the days passed, my hate for you grew. I knew Dre didn't see me like that. My brother made sure I knew it, but I just couldn't grasp it, so I held on. I felt like, if I held on, maybe one day he would see me the same way I saw him. Even when he went away and did that time, I sat back and waited, but as soon as he got out, it was you he was pressed up about. I was the fool. Guess, in a way, I still am."

"No, you're not a fool. You're just a woman who knows what you want. Dre and I clicked when we first met, but I was with Dory, and yes there was an attraction, but not enough to see a future with him. I care about him a lot, but honestly, my heart is not there."

Tasha was shocked at what Shay had revealed and wondered if she had ever told Dre.

"I'm curious to know if you've told Dre how you feel. I mean, it would be wrong to string him along."

"Actually, Dre does know how I feel, and come to find out, he feels the same. What happened between us that night should have never happened, but things got a little out of hand. It took that night for the both of us to realize where we stood. And when you confronted me in there, I know I talked a lot of shit, but Tasha, you got his heart, and if you can't see that, then I don't know what to tell you. And as far as my father goes, he can eat a bullet."

"What? Well, that's funny, because from what I remember, you a daddy's girl. At least that's what it looked like when you packed up and ran away with him. Why the sudden change of heart?"

"I'd love to share, but it's a rather long story."

"Well, it looks like I'm free for the rest of the afternoon, so I have plenty of time to listen."

Chapter 18

Malachi walked into the small efficiency apartment he had been staying in and laid his Ruger on the kitchen counter. The place wasn't much to brag about, and wasn't what he had been used to, but it was what he could afford. It was also a place that no one would think to look for him at.

The suit and tie he had on was a bit uncomfortable, but it had been fitting for the occasion. Mellow's funeral had been nice, and Malachi could tell that Daymion spared no expense on sending his friend home. The only problem was that it should have been Daymion's son in that casket instead. Malachi had watched the funeral from a distance because he couldn't chance being seen. He knew that niggas wanted him dead, and so far, he had managed to escape them.

He still couldn't believe that Mellow had stood in the way of his mission. Malachi had put the gold tip in his gun especially for Dre, but because of Mellow, that mufucka was still walking around with air in his lungs. It had been the perfect opportunity for Malachi, but because of some sort of loyalty to Daymion, Mellow had fucked up the whole plan. Now Malachi would have to wait for another chance to come along.

He pulled his cell phone from the back pocket of his slacks and checked to see if he had missed any calls. Malachi hadn't heard from Shay in days and wondered what was going on with her. He had gotten used to her calling several times a day just to check up on him, but lately, she had been slacking. He was about to dial her number and see what was going on but decided against it because it had gotten late. All Malachi wanted was a shot of liquor and a hot shower, so he could relax. He had thought about going back out so he could pick up one of the young tenders he passed on the corner, but at that moment, Malachi wasn't even sure his dick would get hard.

Malachi poured a small amount of the brown liquor and swished it around the bottom of the glass before he put it to his lips and emptied the contents. The liquor was strong and stung the back of his throat, but not enough to stop him from taking another shot. Malachi slang the glass back a second time and stood still while the brown liquor settled in his stomach. Malachi knew right away that he would regret drinking it, but decided he would enjoy the moment and deal with the repercussions when the time came.

The two straight shots of liquor had Malachi feeling tipsy. He had never been a heavy drinker, so it only took a small amount for him to catch a buzz. When he finally made his way to the bathroom, he stripped and stepped into the steamy, hot water. With his head leaned back, Malachi thought about all the lies he had been living with. Some, he knew, he would never be forgiven for if they were to come out.

He had done some shit in his days, but it was stuff he needed to do, however, no one would ever understand his logic. He would continue to let others believe the stories that had been told because things worked better for him that way. He didn't give a fuck who it had hurt in the process. Malachi's only concern was himself, fuck everyone else.

When Malachi finished his shower, he didn't bother to dry off, instead, he walked to the bedroom bare ass naked, dick swinging and all. He sat down on the twin bed and kicked his feet up. One push of a button and his thirty-inch television clicked on. Malachi flicked from channel to channel but couldn't find anything he wanted to watch, so he threw the remote down on the side of the bed. Malachi thought about the young girl on the corner again and his dick rocked up instantly. It had been a while since he ran up in some good pussy, so he went against his better judgment and got dressed.

When Malachi pulled up on the corner, he spotted the fine young tender standing against the wall by herself. He had never seen her before which was even better, because if he didn't know her, then that meant she didn't know him either. Malachi rolled the passenger side window down and nodded his head at her. Somehow, she knew exactly what the gesture meant because she walked right to his car. Malachi watched as she switched her hips back and forth and hoped that she threw the pussy the same way. His nut sack suddenly felt heavier, and he couldn't wait to empty it. When she leaned over and rested her arms on the door, Malachi could see deep in her cleavage. His hands begin to itch at the thought of holding her juicy breasts while he sucked on her nipples. The anticipation was about to drive him crazy, and he was ready to get the party started.

"Sup, ma? I saw you out here when I passed by earlier and I ain't been able to get you off my mind. What you thing about spending some time with a real nigga?" Malachi smiled and reached in his pocket to pull out a wad of bills.

The female looked at the money and licked her lips. Little did she know, the wad was a bunch of ones. Malachi wasn't the big baller he had been before, so he had to fake it. Luckily, the female fell for it and hopped into the passenger seat. "I guess I am a little lonely out here, and it looks like it's going to be a slow night anyway."

"Don't worry. A nigga like me is about to speed that shit up. What all you into?"

"I'm into anything that pays the bills, so whatever you like, you can get."

Malachi nodded his head and then had to adjust his dick. It was going to be a good night for him, and one he definitely needed. He was glad that he went back and picked her up because he needed to do something that would take his mind off the streets and his money woes. He wondered how the female was going to act once she realized that she hadn't hooked a big fish. Malachi didn't have time for games, so he decided that if the bitch showed out, he would just bust her in the dome and shut her up for good, but if she acted right after he paid her, he would reward her greatly after he bounced back up. He just didn't know how soon that would be.

Chapter 19

"Ya' know, pops, I'm real sorry that Mellow had to die for us to come together like this, and I know it's my fault that we didn't do this sooner. I just wasn't sure what would happen. I couldn't have taken another let down."

"Ya' know, Dreighton, it's all good. We here now and we gonna make the best of all this. Mellow's gone, and ain't shit we can do about it. This right here is what he wanted for us so let's make the best of it. I need you to stop worrying about a let down, because that ain't gonna happen. Let's just find that nigga and get him out the streets."

"I'm with you on that, my nigga. When we gonna hit the block and handle that?"

Daymion and Dre turned to the sound of Kenny's voice and shook their heads. He was dressed in all black with an assault rifle dangling at his side. Kenny had grown tired of mufuckas taking him for a pussy, so he was ready to show the block a different side of him. One they wasn't ready for. He was going to do what he should have done a long time ago, and stand up for Dre. Kenny still felt bad for the way he had done him and was grateful that Dre forgave him, now, he had to pray that Tasha forgave him too. Kenny was ready to step up and fight in any war his people had going on.

Kenny had also talked to Dre about the situation with Shay and was shocked to find out that he saw his future with Tasha. Now, Kenny would have to fix things with Shay too, but if she really felt for him the way she said, it shouldn't be that hard.

"Mufucka, put that gun away while you in my house. If Kayla came in here right now, she would kick your ass outta here. Shit, at least respect her."

"My bad, Day. I'm just ready to make that move."

"Don't worry, it's gonna be made. I already got someone in position to help us out on that. When they're in place, we'll know it and that's when we make our move. Until then, we chill. We don't want anyone else to lose their life."

"What you mean you got somebody on it? Who? We can't afford to let this mufucka get away again. Took him this long to come out of hiding, next time, we may not be so lucky."

"Don't worry about who's on it because I can assure you they'll be successful. In the meantime, we wait for their call and that's when we make our move."

Daymion left the room to go tend to some other business. He had promised Kayla a night out because he had been neglecting her for the drama that had been going on in the streets. The last thing he wanted was for her to be unhappy, so he had to make all the right moves to keep a smile on her face. Once Daymion was gone, Dre needed to let Kenny know where he stood.

"Aye, bruh. Just so you know, me and Shay… we ain't got nothing going on. She ain't where my head is at, or my heart. So, you ain't got to walk away. Stay where you at and build something with her, because I ain't gone be able to."

"Ain't no problem walking away. I don't need shit else to come between us."

"Ain't gone be no problem. I'm in love with Tasha, and when all this shit is over, if I'm still breathing, I plan on making her wifey. She done stood in the mud long enough. It's time for me to clean her feet off and make shit official."

Kenny nodded, but didn't speak at first. He had only wanted Dre to keep it one hundred with Tasha, but he never truly felt like he would. He knew his sister would move heaven and earth to belong to Dre and she had proven her worth.

"Yeah, Dre. I mean, sis done weathered a lot of storms for your ass and I ain't gone lie, I ain't think she would even have a chance with you. I'm glad I was wrong. And Shay, bruh? She is a mufucka, but she's my peace. For you, I would have let her go."

"Well, now you don't have to. Be happy, and never feel like there's some tension between us because we good, and we gone stay that way."

"Bet that, but yo, I gotta make a move real quick. I'll be back."

Kenny held up the assault rifle he had been holding and smiled. He was about to pop the nigga named Jason who had stepped to Daymion at the funeral. Little did Jason know, but Kenny had overheard him talking to another nigga about pulling a jack move on Daymion once he worked himself into the crew. Kenny didn't say anything to Daymion because he figured it was something he could take care of himself. Weaning himself off the crack pipe had made Kenny violent, so mufuckas in the hood better watch they backs.

Dre shook his head, but didn't ask any questions. He didn't want to know about anything that was going down, so he let Kenny go on his way. He figured they could catch up with each other later. Dre leaned back on the plush couch so he could relax his mind, but no sooner than his head hit the cushion than the door opened. Dre looked up just in time to see Tasha walk in, but she wasn't alone. Shay had walked in behind her.

Dre was confused because last he heard Tasha hated Shay, and as far as he knew, that had not changed. He sat up quickly because he felt like some bullshit was about to go down. He hadn't heard anything about them calling a truce and becoming friends, so the shit wasn't adding up, and it caused Dre to get paranoid all over again.

"Sup with this shit here? Last time I checked, you two was enemies. The fuck did that change?"

Tasha put her hands on her hips and looked at Dre while he sat there looking like a deer caught in headlights. She already knew what he was going to have questions when he saw Shay, but little did he know, it was time to squash all the drama between them. Tasha had been so worried about losing him to Shay, when all along, she should have just been chilling.

"Shit changed when we both realized wasn't shit to be enemies for. All this time, I been in my feelings about you and her for no reason. Shay told me everything that I should have heard from you. I just don't understand why I didn't know how you felt. Why you did me like that?"

"Come on now, Tasha, I been trying to show you what it was, but your stubborn ass ain't wanna listen. You were too busy looking for other shit that you wasn't never gone find. Better open up your damn eyes before you miss out."

"Miss out? Nah, nigga, that ain't about to happen because you ain't going nowhere and I ain't about to let nothing else get in the way of us being together."

"Shit, it's about time. A nigga like me was only trying to keep you happy. Ya' feel me?"

"Hmm, I'd be happier if I could feel you right now. Think you could make that happen?"

"I tell you what. When we get home, you can feel a nigga all night. You cool with that?"

"Yeah, I guess I am, but you know I'ma hold you to your word."

Tasha had Dre on swole, and as bad as he wanted to fuck her, he knew that it was not the time or place. It wasn't because of Shay's presence or the fact that they were in his father's house. It was just too much other shit going on to focus on other things. Tasha and Dre almost forgot that Shay was in the room, so she cleared her throat and reminded them of her presence.

"Um, I hate to be a party pooper, but I think maybe I should leave. I need to go find Kenny and hopefully make things good between us too."

Dre stood from the couch and draped an arm around Tasha's shoulders. He forgot that neither Tasha nor Shay knew that him and Kenny had made amends. He didn't want to ruin the mood, but he felt like it was time to put it out there.

"Um, Shay, about Kenny. Me and him, we good now. Shit he did to me wasn't that serious. Matter of fact, the nigga left not too long ago, so if you stick around, you might just run into him."

Tasha gave Dre a confused look and then she looked at Shay, who only shrugged her shoulders in return. Tasha wasn't sure how she would feel by seeing her brother again. A lot of time had passed, and it wasn't that she didn't love him, she just wasn't happy with the way he had done Dre. It had been years since she had seen him, and Tasha knew that her feelings would take over and cause her emotions to spin. No sooner than she began to reminisce, Kenny walked in the door.

"Tasha. It's good to see you, sis."

"Where have you been at, Kenny? Why haven't you ever come back to check on me or at least tried to make things right?"

"I apologize for that, but I was so ashamed of the things I had done and didn't know exactly what to do. I know you been mad at me for how I done Dre. That nigga always looked out and I just stabbed him in the back. I was always worried about him hurting you, but in the end, I was the one who broke your heart. I fucked up, Tasha. I can admit that, but I need you back in my life. I ain't complete without you."

Kenny had his arms open and although Tasha hesitated at first, she ran into them. She had missed him so much and was grateful that they had a chance to make things right. She and Kenny had been through so much and she hated the fact that they had been on the outs, but she had refused to be disloyal to Dre. Thankfully, everything had worked itself out.

Kenny broke his embrace with Tasha and looked at Shay. He had hurt her too, not knowing that he didn't have to. He was just trying to do what he could to make shit right between him and Dre. Kenny looked to his friend and when Dre nodded, he knew it was all good, so Kenny walked over to Shay, but he didn't have to say one word because she welcomed him with open arms.

Dre could see the happiness in Shay's eyes when she looked at Kenny, and he felt a sense of peace. Shit had come together for the good for all of them. Dre was curious though, about how Kenny had left to take a life and got back so quickly, looking as if he ain't do shit wrong. Dre waited until Kenny Shay were done making up and then he walked up to Tasha and put his arms around her. She was all he needed, and he was glad he realized it before it was too late.

"Baby, why don't you and Shay step out for a minute. I need to holla at your brother real quick."

"Okay, but just know that all this time you wasting, you will make up to me."

Tasha smiled and melted Dre's heart all over again. Then she motioned to Shay to follow her. Dre waited until the two of them were gone to ask what he had been dying to know.

"Aye, Kenny, how the hell you went and handle some business and got back so fast?"

"Shiiiit. Nigga, when I was on that pipe, all my senses were heightened and once I got off, it made me feel like superman. Shits crazy, Dre. I move at the mufuckin' speed of light now, or at least it seems like it."

The two of them shared a laugh at the comment and then the room was quiet, both in their own thoughts until finally, Kenny opened another conversation.

"Ya know, Dre, when I hooked up with Shay, it was on some spiteful shit, but it didn't take me long to realize I was really on something else. I was really feeling her. But to have you back in my life, I really would have walked away. You ain't never did me dirty and I 'preciate that."

"Regardless of why you hooked up with her, I ain't on that shit, because I'm where I need to be at. We cool, Kenny, and you ain't got to ever bring up the past. What's done is done. We gone move on like shit ain't never been sweeter."

Before Kenny could respond, Dre's cell rang and startled the two of them. He checked to see who the caller was because he didn't feel like dealing with bullshit. He was in good spirits and wanted to stay that way. But Dre had a funny feeling that Daymion was going to fuck it up.

"Sup, Pops? the hell is you at?"

"I'm on my way back to the house to drop Kayla off and pick you up. If Kenny is still there, tell him to make sure his weapon is fully loaded. We 'bout to blow a mufucka up."

Dre didn't get to ask Daymion any questions because he had hung up on him, but from the anxiousness he heard in Daymion's voice, it had to be something big. Dre looked at Kenny and gave him the message.

"Aye, Kenny, that was pops on the other end. Must have a big fish to fry, because he said to make sure you full and ready."

"What? Now you know a nigga like me stay ready. Where we got to go?"

"I'ont know yet, but he's on the way to pick us up. We'll find out when he gets here."

No sooner than Dre said it, Daymion walked in and went straight to a secret compartment behind a hanging photo. He opened it up and pulled out a Glock and some extra ammo and then reached back in to pull out a nine-millimeter. He shut the compartment back and walked over to Dre, handing him the nine.

"Sup, pop? The hell is we doing all this for?"

Daymion smiled and tucked his gun and then answered the question. "We doing this for Malachi."

Chapter 20

Jakiyah had one of Malachi's nuts in her mouth while she slowly stroked his manhood, and even though what she was doing made her sick on her stomach, she knew she had to pull through. She just hoped the dick was good enough to make it worth her time. She heard Malachi moan in pleasure from above and looked up. He was actually a nice-looking man. It was just his personality that made him ugly.

It was time for the real show to begin and Jakiyah planned on putting up an Oscar worthy performance. She knew how to make a man feel like a King, even when he was a lowly peasant like Malachi. Jakiyah let go of his dick so she could prepare herself, but Malachi had something else in mind.

"Aye, ma, why don't you come up here and take a seat so I can get a little taste of you?"

Jakiyah smiled and lifted up. She loved getting her pussy ate, but never would have thought that Malachi would be the type. She knew that most black men claimed they didn't go down there, when in all actuality, they loved that shit. Jakiyah loved the taste of pussy too, she just preferred the dick.

Jakiyah finally positioned herself over Malachi's face and squatted. As soon as her swollen clit was in reach of his lips, he went to work. Malachi sucked on her pearl so hard it made her dizzy. His head game was the shit and almost made Jakiyah forget why she was there, but thankfully she was still able to focus and enjoy the pleasure he was giving her at the same time.

"Mmm. Malachi, damn, nigga. You know what the hell you doing. Don't stop baby. A bitch is about to cum all over those lips. Yes."

Malachi began to suck harder and faster while Jakiyah rotated her hips. He was enjoying the smell and taste of her, but he was ready to push up in something tight and wet. Malachi heard Jakiyah's moans get louder and when her legs began to shake, he knew she was about to cum. All of a sudden, her creamy juices flowed and ran down his left cheek. She put her hands on the headboard and leaned her head back in complete pleasure. Malachi had done his work and now she would get back to hers.

"Dayum, I think that was the best head I ever got. I ain't know there was a man alive that could eat on pussy like that. I'ma show you just how good it was to me and repay you. I'ma get on that dick and ride it until you lose your mind. You ain't gonna ever want to push that pipe in anybody else. You don't know it, but you done met your match."

Malachi smiled because he loved to fuck bitches that talked shit, and was almost one hundred percent positive that Jakiyah would back up every word. So far, she had proven herself, but Malachi felt like teasing her anyway.

"Ya' know, you talk a lot of shit for a bitch that be out there working the corner."

"Oh baby, it ain't shit I'm talking. I'm stating facts and you 'bout to find that out for yourself."

Jakiyah turned her back to him and positioned herself over his fully erect manhood. She admired his length and thickness and was sure that it was enough to fill her up. She put a hand on each ass cheek and spread them apart while Malachi held his dick straight up like a pole. His mushroom shaped head was already oozing pre-cum so she knew he was good and ready. Luckily her pussy was so wet that she wouldn't need any lubrication. Malachi had made sure of that.

As soon as the head of Malachi's dick touched her entrance, Jakiyah slid down on it and filled herself up. She let go of her ass cheeks so she could reposition her hands on Malachi's thighs. Once she made sure her balance was on point, Jakiyah went to work. She fucked Malachi so good, his eyes rolled into the back of his head, and when he came it was so intense, he felt like he was having a seizure.

When it was all over with, Jakiyah knew it was time to finish what she had started. After Mellow was killed, Daymion had stepped to her to help him set Malachi up. She would have agreed to do anything to avenge Mellow's death, so she stood on that corner every night and waited for Malachi to take the bait. Just like every other man, he had a weakness for pussy, and it was what she would use to get in.

Jakiyah had been Mellow's side piece for years, and although she knew she would never be number one, she rode with him and played her position without any drama. Those nights he had problems with his bitch, he would go to Jakiyah, and she would welcome him with open arms. He had always told her that she was free to do whatever she wanted, but Jakiyah had so much respect for Mellow that she just sat back and chilled, and now that he was gone, she was fucked up.

"Damn, that was some good dick. So good I might just pay you instead. First, I need something to wet my throat. I'm thirsty as hell. I don't want to overstep my boundaries, but do you mind if I grab a glass of water?"

"Nah, ma, go 'head. Grab me one while you at it, though. A nigga has to rehydrate after that."

Jakiyah smiled and got up. As she was getting off the bed, Malachi slapped her on the ass. She didn't mind, though, because it would be the last ass he would ever slap. She was going to make sure of that.

Jakiyah walked out of the bedroom and into the small kitchen and pulled two glasses from the cabinet. She opened the refrigerator in hopes of finding a jug of water, but it was bare. She had never been fond of drinking water straight from the faucet, but desperate times called for desperate measures and that night, she would make an exception. She turned the cold water on and filled the glasses. She was so thirsty she drank hers and had to refill it. When she was done, she opened the charm that hung around her neck, a gift from Mellow, and emptied its contents into the water she would give Malachi to drink and then she walked back to the bedroom.

Malachi was still in the same position she had left him in, so she passed him the glass and sat down beside him. She guzzled the second glass she had made for herself, although she knew she would be pissing like crazy later. She was just ready to get the shit she was doing over with.

Jakiyah noticed that Malachi only sipped the water, but she needed him to drink it down. He was going to drink that water one way or the other. Jakiyah would make sure of it. She sat her empty glass down and picked his semi hard dick up. Jakiyah got between Malachi's legs and teased the head of his manhood, and then looked up at him. Without saying a word, Malachi drank the water down and then put his hands on the back of her head. He was ready for round two and didn't want to waste another minute.

"Come on, ma. Go 'head and do what you do best. You get him back right and he's gone reward you real good."

Jakiyah put her lips around his width and before she got to the base of his length, she felt his body go limp.

Chapter 21

Daymion and Dre were on their way to the address Jakiyah had sent with Kenny following close behind. If things went according to plan, Malachi would finally get what he deserved. So far, the ride had been quiet because each of them were lost in their own thoughts. However, Dre became curious about the situation and asked what he felt he should have already known.

"Hol' up, pops. Who the hell is Jakiyah and what exactly does she have to do with Malachi?"

"Jakiyah was one of Mellow's side chicks and it's because of her that we are within arm's reach of Malachi. I couldn't think of any other way to trip him up, so I put some pussy in view and he fell for it. Other than that, Jakiyah ain't got shit to do with him."

"Well, I hope you for sure about that because I'm kinda tired of making dry runs. I'm ready to wet that mufucka up."

"Don't worry, son. With Jakiyah involved, it's always a sure thing."

Dre nodded his head and leaned back so he could get his mind right before he faced Malachi. He couldn't believe that after all that time he was about to look the devil in the eyes once again. Dre thought about all the shit Malachi had put him and his mom through and knew that he could not go unpunished. He wanted to make sure the mufucka suffered in the worst kind of way.

When Daymion finally pulled into the shabby looking apartment complex, he understood why Malachi would have chosen it. No one could have ever guessed that the so-called king pen would live in such a manner. Daymion wondered if there was more to it, though.

Daymion cut his lights and parked around the back of the complex. He didn't know much about the area so he couldn't afford to take any chances. He had only gone there to take one life, so he hoped there were no witnesses creeping around. Kayla would never understand if he had to go back in on a murder rap. As soon as Kenny backed up in the spot beside them, Daymion and Dre got out.

"What's the word, Daymion? I'm ready to blow a mufuckin' gasket in somebody's head."

"Don't worry, Kenny. We'll have plenty of time for that, but right now, I just need you to stand guard on the outside while me and Dre shake that nigga up."

"I got you, bruh. Consider it done." Kenny held his shooter up for special effects and followed behind Daymion and Dre. That was his chance to prove his loyalty to Dre, and to show him that he had his back for real.

Daymion walked up the stairs that led to the apartment. Once he was in front of it, he looked back at Dre and Kenny and nodded. He knew Dre was anxious because he had been waiting on that day to arrive. Malachi had to be eliminated because as long as he was breathing, they would all have to continue to look over their shoulders, and they had grown tired of living that way.

Daymion pulled out his phone and sent a short text to Jakiyah. No sooner than he put his phone back in his pocket she opened the door and let them in. Kenny got a good look at her before she closed the door back and had to grab his dick to settle it. Th bitch was fine and if it wasn't for Shay, he would have tried to put something in her life.

"He's in the bedroom, but you don't have to worry; he ain't going anywhere. I made sure that I fucked him real good and I doubled up on the crushed pills. He'll be out for a while."

"Thanks, Jakiyah. You can go now, and here's a little something for your trouble."

Jakiyah looked at the stack of bills in Daymion's hand and shook her head. "No, Daymion, that's not why I did it. It was for Mellow. You can keep your cash; I don't need it. Mellow had me set up real good, and to accept that money would make me feel like I've disrespected his memory."

Jakiyah turned to leave but not before she got a good look at Dre. She lifted her brow and smiled, but that was the most she would do. She could tell by the look in his eyes and his demeanor that he was going to be major in the game one day. She just hoped the game didn't take him out before then.

Once Jakiyah was gone, Daymion and Dre walked into the bedroom and saw Malachi tied up to the bed post. Daymion was thankful that Jakiyah at least had the decency to put some clothes on him before she left him that way. Malachi looked to be in a deep sleep and would stay that way until the drugs wore off. In the meantime, Daymion and Dre searched the apartment but only found a handful of money. Daymion wondered why it was such a small amount, but he would worry about that later.

Dre sat impatiently as the hours passed. He was ready to bash Malachi's skull in but he wanted to do it while the nigga was fully alert so he could feel every ounce of pain Dre lashed upon him. His mother had suffered on a daily basis at the hands of Malachi, and it was time for some payback. Dre just wished she was there to see the mufucka suffer too.

"Damn, pops. The hell did that bitch give him? He been out for hours and I'm tired of waiting. I'm ready to show his pussy ass what's up."

"Come on, son, just chill. We finally have him where we want him and that's what matters most. He's in our hands now and he ain't getting away this time. Shit, we already waited this long."

"Yeah, you right, but now that the time is here, I'm anxious as a mufucka. You can't feel like I feel because you wasn't there. You ain't a witness to all the shitty things he did to Momma. I'll be the first to admit that she wasn't perfect by a long shot, but she ain't deserve to be treated like that. Fuck nigga gotta pay his dues now."

"And he's going to, Dre. You gone have a chance to pay him back for everything. You got my word on that."

Dre nodded and became silent. He just needed a minute to dig into his mental because he had a lot of shit to get off his chest. There was something he needed to say to Daymion that had been long overdue, and he felt like it was the perfect time, but first, he pulled out a blunt and lit it. He felt like the weed would help his words flow a little easier, but as soon as the stench hit Daymion, Dre's words would be cut short.

"When the hell you start smoking weed? Shit right there ain't cool, especially at a time like this. I need your mind to be right."

"My mind stays right. This just enhances it a little more. Besides, there's a whole lot you don't know about me."

"Yeah, well maybe when this is over, we can catch up on each other."

Before Dre had a chance to respond, he heard a low moan come from Malachi. Daymion and Dre both stood and stepped to the end of the bed he lay upon. They wanted to be in his line of vision as soon as he opened his eyes, because they wanted him to know that they would be the last two people he would ever see.

Dre suddenly pulled his weapon and aimed it at Malachi. He was ready to pull the trigger on the mufucka that took his momma from him, but Daymion held his hand up and stopped him. Dre gave his father a look of death because he couldn't understand why he would stop him from blasting a hole in the nigga that took his whole life from him. Shit just wasn't making any sense.

"The fuck is you stopping me for? Let me go 'head and blast this nigga."

Daymion nodded his head toward the room door where Shay stood with a blank stare in her eyes. As soon as Dre saw her, he lowered his weapon. There was no way he could kill her father in front of her. Dre was about to ask her how she got in, but then he remembered that it was Kenny guarding the door and he would have broken all the rules for her. At one time, Dre would have done the same, but all that had changed when he realized who really held his heart.

"Please, Dre. I know how much you hate him, but don't kill him. Not just yet."

Dre and Daymion were confused but Malachi understood her just fine. He would have played dumb and begged her to save him, but the powder Jakiyah had put in his drink had left him unable to form the words. The most he could do was grunt and moan but soon he wouldn't even be doing that. Dre couldn't understand what was going on because last he checked Shay had abandoned everybody for Malachi and now she seemed to take pleasure in knowing his life would be over soon.

"Shay? What the hell you doing here? I hope you don't think you 'bout to stop his execution, because this mufucka is going to die today."

"I'm aware of the fact that you and countless others want my father dead, but I don't want you to take that pleasure from me. I'm the one who owes him, and he knows it. Don't you, daddy?"

The tears began to form in Malachi's eyes proving that he was still a pussy, but Shay had no sympathy for him. He thought he had spent all his money carelessly, but Shay had wiped out his funds. He wouldn't be needing them anyway because she planned to send him straight to hell.

"Do you want to enlighten us on what the hell is going on here, because this shit ain't making no damn sense."

"Yes, Daymion, I would love to tell you about my so-called father here, with his broke ass, thanks to me. When I found out that it was really him that killed my mother, I slowly began to take every penny he had until there was hardly anything left, and then, just like you I started making plans to eliminate him."

"Wait. Hold up, because you're not making any sense to me right now. We all know that I was the one who fired that shot that killed your mother. It was meant for Dory, but because of him pulling her in as a shield, it struck her instead."

"No, that's what you believed happened, and yes, you did fire a shot, but you didn't kill her, he did. My father was there and he waited until he saw you pointing that gun. When you pulled the trigger, he did too, but you missed, Daymion. Your bullet shattered the window, but his, the bullet that was meant for my mother, came from him and hit its target."

"Where did you get all of this information from, because I know he didn't give it to you."

Shay turned and looked at Malachi with saddened eyes. She had began to grow detached to him when she found out the truth, but even as evil as he was he had been good to her and loved her as if she had always been in his life. As soon as Shay found out Malachi pulled the trigger on her mother, she began plotting. Her first step had been moving out of his house because being around him made her sick on her stomach. There was no way she could have faced him everyday after finding out what he had done.

"I overheard him talking to my uncle one night. Unc asked him if he would ever tell me the truth about my mother getting killed because he felt like I needed to know the truth. My father told him that he was going to carry the secret to the grave and that I should keep believing it was you, Daymion. He said it was better for me to hate you than to hate him. And as much as I don't want to admit it, I don't hate him either, but I also don't love him enough to let him live."

Dre listened to everything Shay had said but she had to know that she wasn't about to steal his joy. He had wanted to put a bullet in Malachi's dome for the longest and he would succeed one way or the other.

"So, you think you just gonna come in here and take from me what I've wanted for so long? Shit there ain't about to happen. I'm the one that had to watch my momma get beaten and raped on a nightly basis. That bastard had her so strung out she couldn't think straight. I owe him for that and I'm gonna pay his ass. Not you or anyone else, but me."

"Dre, I know what your momma went through. Everyday I looked in your eyes, I saw not only your pain but the pain you also carried for her. I owe him too, though. He took my momma, too. This ain't just your battle, it's mine."

Dre and Shay stood and stared at each other. Each one wanted their revenge on the enemy, and no matter who fired the first shot, they knew that Malachi had to go. The cemetery gates were open and waiting on him so he could begin his journey to hell.

They could hear Malachi on the bed still trying to speak words that no one cared to listen to. There wasn't one thing he could say that would save him from the wrath of those he had hurt the most. Malachi knew he was a dead man, and he was ready for whatever they brought.

Daymion got in between his son and Shay. To be honest, Malachi owed all three of them his life so he felt that all of them should have a shot, but first he had to stop them from arguing about it.

"Hold up. Y'all standing in this mufuckin' room arguing over a bitch ass nigga that owes all of us. Nigga should have been dead. I got a solution, though. I say since we all want a piece, we all take a piece."

Dre and Shay agreed with what Daymion had said and pulled their weapons out. When all three of them turned to look Malachi in the face, he laughed at them which only made them angrier. Daymion shrugged and pulled his weapon too. It was time to eliminate the opposition and get all their lives back.

"Y'all ready for this?" Daymion asked and smiled, and then on the count of three all of them fired their guns, putting an end to Malachi Jensen, sending him where he belonged. Right through cemetery gates.

Lock Down Publications and Ca$h Presents
Assisted Publishing Packages

BASIC PACKAGE	UPGRADED PACKAGE
$499	$800
Editing	Typing
Cover Design	Editing
Formatting	Cover Design
	Formatting
ADVANCE PACKAGE	**LDP SUPREME PACKAGE**
$1,200	$1,500
Typing	Typing
Editing	Editing
Cover Design	Cover Design
Formatting	Formatting
Copyright registration	Copyright registration
Proofreading	Proofreading
Upload book to Amazon	Set up Amazon account
	Upload book to Amazon
	Advertise on LDP, Amazon and
	Facebook Page

***Other services available upon request.
Additional charges may apply

Lock Down Publications
P.O. Box 944
Stockbridge, GA 30281-9998
Phone: 470 303-9761

Submission Guideline

Submit the first three chapters of your completed manuscript to ldpsubmissions@gmail.com. In the subject line add **Your Book's Title**. The manuscript must be in a Word Doc file and sent as an attachment. Document should be in Times New Roman, double spaced, and in size 12 font. Also, provide your synopsis and full contact information. If sending multiple submissions, they must each be in a separate email.

Have a story but no way to send it electronically? You can still submit to LDP/Ca$h Presents. Send in the first three chapters, written or typed, of your completed manuscript to:

LDP: Submissions Dept
P.O. Box 944
Stockbridge, GA 30281-9998

DO NOT send original manuscript. Must be a duplicate. Provide your synopsis and a cover letter containing your full contact information.

Thanks for considering LDP and Ca$h Presents.

NEW RELEASES

BLOODLINE OF A SAVAGE 1&2
THESE VICIOUS STREETS 1&2
RELENTLESS GOON
RELENTLESS GOON 2
BY PRINCE A. TAUHID

THE BUTTERFLY MAFIA 1-3
BY FUMIYA PAYNE

A THUG'S STREET PRINCESS 1&2
BY MEESHA

CITY OF SMOKE 2
BY MOLOTTI

STEPPERS 1,2&3
THE REAL BADDIES OF CHI-RAQ
BY KING RIO

THE LANE 1&2
BY KEN-KEN SPENCE

THUG OF SPADES 1&2
LOVE IN THE TRENCHES 2
CORNER BOYS
BY COREY ROBINSON

TIL DEATH 3
BY ARYANNA

THE BIRTH OF A GANGSTER 4
BY DELMONT PLAYER

PRODUCT OF THE STREETS 1&2
BY DEMOND "MONEY" ANDERSON

NO TIME FOR ERROR
BY KEESE

MONEY HUNGRY DEMONS
BY TRANAY ADAMS

Coming Soon from Lock Down Publications/Ca$h Presents

IF YOU CROSS ME ONCE 6
ANGEL V
By Anthony Fields

IMMA DIE BOUT MINE 5
By Aryanna

A THUGS STREET PRINCESS 3
By Meesha

PRODUCT OF THE STREETS 3
By Demond Money Anderson

CORNER BOYS 2
By Corey Robinson

THE MURDER QUEENS 6&7
By Michael Gallon

CITY OF SMOKE 3
By Molotti

CONFESSIONS OF A DOPE BOY
By Nicholas Lock

THA TAKEOVER
By Keith Chandler

BETRAYAL OF A G 2
By Ray Vinci

CRIME BOSS
By Playa Ray

155

Available Now

RESTRAINING ORDER 1 & 2
By **CA$H & Coffee**

LOVE KNOWS NO BOUNDARIES 1-3
By **Coffee**

RAISED AS A GOON I, II, III & IV
BRED BY THE SLUMS I, II, III
BLAST FOR ME I & II
ROTTEN TO THE CORE I II III
A BRONX TALE I, II, III
DUFFLE BAG CARTEL I II III IV V VI
HEARTLESS GOON I II III IV V
A SAVAGE DOPEBOY I II
DRUG LORDS I II III
CUTTHROAT MAFIA I II
KING OF THE TRENCHES
By **Ghost**

LAY IT DOWN I & II
LAST OF A DYING BREED I II
BLOOD STAINS OF A SHOTTA I & II III
By **Jamaica**

LOYAL TO THE GAME I II III
LIFE OF SIN I, II III
By **TJ & Jelissa**

IF LOVING HIM IS WRONG…I & II
LOVE ME EVEN WHEN IT HURTS I II III
By **Jelissa**

PUSH IT TO THE LIMIT
By **Bre' Hayes**

BLOODY COMMAS I & II
SKI MASK CARTEL I, II & III
KING OF NEW YORK I II, III IV V
RISE TO POWER I II III
COKE KINGS I II III IV V
BORN HEARTLESS I II III IV
KING OF THE TRAP I II
By **T.J. Edwards**

WHEN THE STREETS CLAP BACK I & II III
THE HEART OF A SAVAGE I II III IV
MONEY MAFIA I II
LOYAL TO THE SOIL I II III
By **Jibril Williams**

A DISTINGUISHED THUG STOLE MY HEART I II & III
LOVE SHOULDN'T HURT I II III IV
RENEGADE BOYS 1-4
PAID IN KARMA 1-3
SAVAGE STORMS 1-3
AN UNFORESEEN LOVE 1-3
BABY, I'M WINTERTIME COLD 1-3
A THUG'S STREET PRINCESS 1&2
By **Meesha**

A GANGSTER'S CODE 1-3
A GANGSTER'S SYN 1-3
THE SAVAGE LIFE 1-3
CHAINED TO THE STREETS 1-3
BLOOD ON THE MONEY 1-3
A GANGSTA'S PAIN 1-3
BEAUTIFUL LIES AND UGLY TRUTHS
CHURCH IN THESE STREETS
By **J-Blunt**

CUM FOR ME 1-8
An LDP Erotica Collaboration

BLOOD OF A BOSS 1-5
SHADOWS OF THE GAME
TRAP BASTARD
By **Askari**

THE STREETS BLEED MURDER 1-3
THE HEART OF A GANGSTA 1-3
By **Jerry Jackson**

WHEN A GOOD GIRL GOES BAD
By **Adrienne**

THE COST OF LOYALTY 1-3
By **Kweli**

BRIDE OF A HUSTLA 1-3
THE FETTI GIRLS 1-3
CORRUPTED BY A GANGSTA 1-4
BLINDED BY HIS LOVE
THE PRICE YOU PAY FOR LOVE 1-3
DOPE GIRL MAGIC 1-3
By **Destiny Skai**

A KINGPIN'S AMBITION
A KINGPIN'S AMBITION II
I MURDER FOR THE DOUGH
By **Ambitious**

TRUE SAVAGE 1-7
DOPE BOY MAGIC 1-3
MIDNIGHT CARTEL 1-3
CITY OF KINGZ 1&2
NIGHTMARE ON SILENT AVE
THE PLUG OF LIL MEXICO 1&2
CLASSIC CITY
By **Chris Green**

A GANGSTER'S REVENGE 1-4
THE BOSS MAN'S DAUGHTERS 1-5
A SAVAGE LOVE 1&2
BAE BELONGS TO ME 1&2
A HUSTLER'S DECEIT 1-3
WHAT BAD BITCHES DO 1-3
SOUL OF A MONSTER 1-3
KILL ZONE
A DOPE BOY'S QUEEN 1-3
TIL DEATH 1-3
IMMA DIE BOUT MINE 1-4
By **Aryanna**

A DOPEBOY'S PRAYER
By **Eddie "Wolf" Lee**

THE KING CARTEL 1-3
By **Frank Gresham**

THESE NIGGAS AIN'T LOYAL 1-3
By **Nikki Tee**

GANGSTA SHYT 1-3
By **CATO**

THE ULTIMATE BETRAYAL
By **Phoenix**

BOSS'N UP 1-3
By **Royal Nicole**

I LOVE YOU TO DEATH
By **Destiny J**

I RIDE FOR MY HITTA
I STILL RIDE FOR MY HITTA
By **Misty Holt**

LOVE & CHASIN' PAPER
By **Qay Crockett**

TO DIE IN VAIN
SINS OF A HUSTLA
By **ASAD**

BROOKLYN HUSTLAZ
By **Boogsy Morina**

BROOKLYN ON LOCK 1 & 2
By **Sonovia**

GANGSTA CITY
By **Teddy Duke**

A DRUG KING AND HIS DIAMOND 1-3
A DOPEMAN'S RICHES
HER MAN, MINE'S TOO 1&2
CASH MONEY HO'S
THE WIFEY I USED TO BE 1&2
PRETTY GIRLS DO NASTY THINGS
By **Nicole Goosby**

LIPSTICK KILLAH 1-3
CRIME OF PASSION 1-3
FRIEND OR FOE 1-3
By **Mimi**

TRAPHOUSE KING 1-3
KINGPIN KILLAZ 1-3
STREET KINGS 1&2
PAID IN BLOOD 1&2
CARTEL KILLAZ 1-3
DOPE GODS 1&2
By **Hood Rich**

THE STREETS ARE CALLING
By **Duquie Wilson**

STEADY MOBBN' 1-3
THE STREETS STAINED MY SOUL 1-3
By **Marcellus Allen**

WHO SHOT YA 1-3
SON OF A DOPE FIEND 1-4
HEAVEN GOT A GHETTO 1&2
SKI MASK MONEY 1&2
By **Renta**

GORILLAZ IN THE BAY 1-4
TEARS OF A GANGSTA 1/&2
3X KRAZY 1&2
STRAIGHT BEAST MODE 1&2
By **DE'KARI**

TRIGGADALE 1-3
MURDA WAS THE CASE 1-3
By **Elijah R. Freeman**

SLAUGHTER GANG 1-3
RUTHLESS HEART 1-3
By **Willie Slaughter**

GOD BLESS THE TRAPPERS 1-3
THESE SCANDALOUS STREETS 1-3
FEAR MY GANGSTA 1-5
THESE STREETS DON'T LOVE NOBODY 1-2
BURY ME A G 1-5
A GANGSTA'S EMPIRE 1-4
THE DOPEMAN'S BODYGAURD 1&2
THE REALEST KILLAZ 1-3
THE LAST OF THE OGS 1-3
By **Tranay Adams**

MARRIED TO A BOSS 1-3
By **Destiny Skai & Chris Green**

KINGZ OF THE GAME 1-7
CRIME BOSS 1-3
By **Playa Ray**

FUK SHYT
By **Blakk Diamond**

DON'T F#CK WITH MY HEART 1&2
By **Linnea**

ADDICTED TO THE DRAMA 1-3
IN THE ARM OF HIS BOSS
By **Jamila**

LOYALTY AIN'T PROMISED 1&2
By **Keith Williams**

YAYO 1-4
A SHOOTER'S AMBITION 1&2
BRED IN THE GAME
By **S. Allen**

TRAP GOD 1-3
RICH $AVAGE 1-3
MONEY IN THE GRAVE 1-3
CARTEL MONEY
By **Martell Troublesome Bolden**

FOREVER GANGSTA 1&2
GLOCKS ON SATIN SHEETS 1&2
By **Adrian Dulan**

TOE TAGZ 1-4
LEVELS TO THIS SHYT 1&2
IT'S JUST ME AND YOU
By **Ah'Million**

KINGPIN DREAMS 1-3
RAN OFF ON DA PLUG
By **Paper Boi Rari**

THE STREETS MADE ME 1-3
By **Larry D. Wright**

CONFESSIONS OF A GANGSTA 1-4
CONFESSIONS OF A JACKBOY 1-3
CONFESSIONS OF A HITMAN
By **Nicholas Lock**

I'M NOTHING WITHOUT HIS LOVE
SINS OF A THUG
TO THE THUG I LOVED BEFORE
A GANGSTA SAVED XMAS
IN A HUSTLER I TRUST
By **Monet Dragun**

QUIET MONEY 1-3
THUG LIFE 1-3
EXTENDED CLIP 1&2
A GANGSTA'S PARADISE
By **Trai'Quan**

CAUGHT UP IN THE LIFE 1-3
THE STREETS NEVER LET GO 1-3
By **Robert Baptiste**

NEW TO THE GAME 1-3
MONEY, MURDER & MEMORIES 1-3
By **Malik D. Rice**

CREAM 2-3
THE STREETS WILL TALK
By **Yolanda Moore**

THE STREETS WILL NEVER CLOSE 1-3
By **K'ajji**

LIFE OF A SAVAGE 1-4
A GANGSTA'S QUR'AN 1-4
MURDA SEASON 1-3
GANGLAND CARTEL 1-3
CHI'RAQ GANGSTAS 1-4
KILLERS ON ELM STREET 1-3
JACK BOYZ N DA BRONX 1-3
A DOPEBOY'S DREAM 1-3
JACK BOYS VS DOPE BOYS 1-3
COKE GIRLZ
COKE BOYS
SOSA GANG 1&2
BRONX SAVAGES
BODYMORE KINGPINS
BLOOD OF A GOON
By **Romell Tukes**

CONCRETE KILLA 1-3
VICIOUS LOYALTY 1-3
By **Kingpen**

THE ULTIMATE SACRIFICE 1-6
KHADIFI
IF YOU CROSS ME ONCE 1-3
ANGEL 1-4
IN THE BLINK OF AN EYE
By **Anthony Fields**

THE LIFE OF A HOOD STAR
By **Ca$h & Rashia Wilson**

NIGHTMARES OF A HUSTLA 1-3
BLOOD AND GAMES 1&2
By **King Dream**

GHOST MOB
By **Stilloan Robinson**

HARD AND RUTHLESS 1&2
MOB TOWN 251
THE BILLIONAIRE BENTLEYS 1-3
REAL G'S MOVE IN SILENCE
By **Von Diesel**

MOB TIES 1-7
SOUL OF A HUSTLER, HEART OF A KILLER 1-3
GORILLAZ IN THE TRENCHES
By **SayNoMore**

BODYMORE MURDERLAND 1-3
THE BIRTH OF A GANGSTER 1-4
By **Delmont Player**

FOR THE LOVE OF A BOSS 1&2
By **C. D. Blue**

KILLA KOUNTY 1-5
By **Khufu**

MOBBED UP 1-4
THE BRICK MAN 1-5
THE COCAINE PRINCESS 1-10
STEPPERS 1-3
SUPER GREMLIN 1-4
By **King Rio**

MONEY GAME 1&2
By **Smoove Dolla**

A GANGSTA'S KARMA 1-4
By **FLAME**

KING OF THE TRENCHES 1-3
By **GHOST & TRANAY ADAMS**

THUG OF SPADES 3 | COREY ROBINSON

QUEEN OF THE ZOO 1&2
By **Black Migo**

GRIMEY WAYS 1-3
BETRAYAL OF A G
By **Ray Vinci**

XMAS WITH AN ATL SHOOTER
By **Ca$h & Destiny Skai**

KING KILLA 1&2
By **Vincent "Vitto" Holloway**

BETRAYAL OF A THUG 1&2
By **Fre$h**

THE MURDER QUEENS 1-5
By **Michael Gallon**

FOR THE LOVE OF BLOOD 1-4
By **Jamel Mitchell**

HOOD CONSIGLIERE 1&2
NO TIME FOR ERROR
By **Keese**

PROTÉGÉ OF A LEGEND 1&2
LOVE IN THE TRENCHES 1&2
By **Corey Robinson**

THE PLUG'S RUTHLESS DAUGHTER
By **Tony Daniels**

BORN IN THE GRAVE 1-3
CRIME PAYS
By **Self Made Tay**

MOAN IN MY MOUTH
By **XTASY**

166

TORN BETWEEN A GANGSTER AND A GENTLEMAN
By **J-BLUNT & Miss Kim**

LOYALTY IS EVERYTHING 1-3
CITY OF SMOKE 1&2
By **Molotti**

HERE TODAY GONE TOMORROW 1&2
By **Fly Rock**

WOMEN LIE MEN LIE 1-4
FIFTY SHADES OF SNOW 1-3
STACK BEFORE YOU SPLURGE
GIRLS FALL LIKE DOMINOES
NAÏVE TO THE STREETS
By **ROY MILLIGAN**

PILLOW PRINCESS
By **S. Hawkins**

THE BUTTERFLY MAFIA 1-3
SALUTE MY SAVAGERY 1&2
By **Fumiya Payne**

THE LANE 1&2
By Ken-Ken Spence

THE PUSSY TRAP 1-5
By **Nene Capri**

DIRTY DNA
By **Blaque**

SANCTIFIED AND HORNY
by **XTASY**

BOOKS BY LDP'S CEO, CA$H

TRUST IN NO MAN
TRUST IN NO MAN 2
TRUST IN NO MAN 3
BONDED BY BLOOD
SHORTY GOT A THUG
THUGS CRY
THUGS CRY 2
THUGS CRY 3
TRUST NO BITCH
TRUST NO BITCH 2
TRUST NO BITCH 3
TIL MY CASKET DROPS
RESTRAINING ORDER
RESTRAINING ORDER 2
IN LOVE WITH A CONVICT
LIFE OF A HOOD STAR
XMAS WITH AN ATL SHOOTER

www.ingramcontent.com/pod-product-compliance
Lightning Source LLC
Chambersburg PA
CBHW060419260626
47161CB00005B/1695